DATE

MR. SEPTEMBER

to Margaret

A novel of South Africa

MR. SEPTEMBER

by
John Trengove

Beaufort Books, Inc.
NEW YORK   TORONTO

Cataloguing in Publication Data

Trengove, John.
Mr. September

ISBN 0-8253-0018-5

I. Title

PS8589.R46M57   813'.5'4   C79-094129-5

First published in the United States in 1980 by
Beaufort Books, Inc., New York.

Printed in Canada

ISBN 0-8253-0018-5

Preface

On a particularly cold, damp, foggy day in the English autumn of 1976, I sat opposite two men in bowler hats on the 9:05 commuter train from Haywards Heath to Victoria Station. We were traversing the depressing squalor of mile upon mile of dilapidated industry and terraced slums which herald the outskirts of Greater London, when one of the men spoke to his companion.

"Awfully bad show . . . whole thing is going to end in a bloodbath."

The younger man lifted his eyebrows to peer at the other's newspaper. "Absolutely inevitable, old boy. Serves these Dutchmen right actually . . . just can't get away with that sort of thing."

"Pity," the older man said. "I recall a South African . . . during the last show, you know . . . flew for the squadron actually. Got the D.F.C. Splendid fellow on a party . . . had a sort of Dutch name."

He extended his arms and turned his newspaper inside out with a practiced flick. I saw the headlines:

"RIOTS IN JOHANNESBURG. THIRTY KILLED."

Despair overwhelmed me. Despair of the terrible illusion of progress which beguiles mankind. Despair of the ever-increasing barrage of printed dailies, weeklies, analyses and commentaries, reinforced by radio, television and film, which left these two informed and probably decent men so punch-drunk with information as to be totally out of touch with reality. What did they really know about the complex history of South Africa?

Should I lean across and tell them about a junior executive, as they would know him, walking enthusiastically through the streets of Amsterdam three centuries ago?

*　　　*　　　*

It was in 1652 that Jan Riebeek set sail from Amsterdam with directions to establish and fortify a victualing station for ships of the Dutch East India Company at the southernmost tip of Africa.

On his arrival at Table Bay, van Riebeek encountered indigenous Hottentots, a yellow-skinned Hamitic tribe of pastoral nomads. Although baffled by European culture, the Hottentots offered rather less resentment and resistance than contemporary Europe or America might afford an immigrant today.

Van Riebeek built his fort, cultivated a garden, bartered longhorned cattle with the Hottentots and kept his accounts. The seed of a new nation was sown.

Slowly, painfully slowly, the tiny settlement grew. To economize while maintaining production and ensuring security, the Council of Seventeen in Amsterdam made grants of land to demobilized mercenaries and retiring Company officials. In 1690 a party of French Huguenots arrived. Contrary to popular belief, the founding fathers were not predominately Dutch. An early census reveals that 40% were German, 27% French, 22% Dutch, and 9% of miscellaneous European origin.

In time the Company imported Malay slaves as well as East Indian convict labor. These coalesced to form the nucleus of yet another unique race, the Cape Colored — a vital, warm, prolific people of mixed Batavian, Hottentot,

Indian and Bushman stock, well laced with a constant infusion of European genes. They were to become the craftsmen, fishermen and laborers of the Cape. In the social alchemy of the colony they evolved a delicate sort of upstairs-downstairs relationship of mutual respect and affection with their white compatriots. Proud of their heritage, the Cape Coloreds were, on later exposure, to develop a profound contempt for blacks who entered their domain. To a Cape Colored, "Kaffir" is the ultimate insult.

But land in the valleys between the towering volcanic peaks around Cape Town, although suited to the vine, was scarce. In search of new grazing, a steady trickle of newcomers, sons, and sons of sons crossed the formidable bastion of the mountains. Except for an abundance of game and roving bands of Hottentots and Bushmen, they found the hinterland empty. But grazing was subject to unpredictable rainfall often punctuated by grinding drought. As a consequence the *trekboer* evolved — a rugged, proudly self-reliant individualist, tempered by hardship and attuned to the land, who moved ever deeper into the wilderness, oblivious to the social and cultural revolutions which swept Europe during the 18th and 19th centuries. In splendid isolation the Boer maintained his standards by an uncompromising Calvinistic adherence to the Old Testament.

Under such circumstances it was not unnatural that a new language should evolve. Afrikaans is a patois based on 17th century Dutch and Teutonic German, enriched by French, Hottentot, Malay and even some English derivatives, and molded by usage to the life of an isolated pastoral society.

With changing fortunes in Europe and colonial rivalry, the Dutch East India Company declined. Successively the Cape of Good Hope came under Dutch, English, French, Dutch again, and finally, in 1806, English control. Unlike the remote Boers of the hinterland, the citizens of Cape Town and those within easy reach of the port were exposed to continual European influences, a circumstance which to

7

this day accounts for differences in character and attitude which distinguish the Cape South African from his compatriots in the Transvaal.

The new English colonial policy was aggressive. English replaced Dutch as the official language; new taxes were levied. The Boer settlers in the eastern extremities of the colony had just encountered a southward migration of blacks. The settlers, with their highly efficient commando system, needed neither help nor advice in dealing with the raids of predatory blacks. But the mischievous politicking of the London Missionary Society induced the colonial office to make retaliation or even adequate defense against the blacks illegal.

In 1820, in pursuit of the new objective of a British dominion in South Africa, 5000 British settlers were dumped on the windswept beaches of Algoa Bay. After a brief exposure to the wilderness they soon shared the discontent of the original Boer settlers.

Then, in 1834, Britain, in "one of its periodic fits of morality," as Macaulay has it, emancipated all the slaves in the Empire. Vagrancy among the freed and hungry slaves presented a new threat. Life became intolerable for the settlers. They were faced with three choices: endure, fight, or leave.

Under almost identical circumstances, the Americans chose to fight. The Boers trekked, moving farther inland north and east. How closely their Declaration of Intent resembles the American Declaration of Independence:

February 2, 1837

As we desire to stand high in the estimation of our brethren, and are anxious that we and the world at large should believe us incapable of severing that sacred tie which binds a Christian to his native soil, without the most sufficient reasons, we are induced to record the following summary of our motives for taking so important a step, and also

8

our intentions respecting our proceedings toward the native tribes which we may meet beyond the boundary.

We quit this colony under the full assurance that the English government has nothing more to require of us, and will allow us to govern ourselves without its interference in the future.

It was their Exodus. They loaded their women and children into wagons, rounded up their cattle, and crossed the Orange River to establish the Orange Free State. Some pressed on northeastward to establish the Transvaal Republic. The Transvaalers sought peace and coexistence with the Zulus; their leader, Piet Retief (a signatory of the Manifesto of Departure from the Cape Colony) was invited to parley. Except for Retief's thirteen-year-old son, who escaped, the whole unarmed delegation was butchered by the Zulu chief Dingaan. Finally in the epic Battle of Blood River the Transvaalers broke the Zulu might.

But independence was not yet theirs. In 1880 Britain attacked the Transvaal, and at Majuba Hill the Boers routed the British in one of the most pathetic debacles in the history of warfare. The independence of Transvaal seemed confirmed.

Then gold was discovered. Hordes of European prospectors, adventurers, and entrepreneurs descended on the Transvaal. The Boers resented both the intrusion and the manner of the intruders. In 1898, after the infamous Jameson Raid on the Transvaal, the whole might of the British Empire was turned on the tiny Boer republic. The Orange Free State came out in support. The second Boer War was declared.

After two years of ridiculous military bungling and catastrophic loss of British lives, the Boer army was crushed by sheer numbers. But the Boers scorned surrender. Mounted guerrilla commandos, not the least notable band led by General Jan Christiaan Smuts, continued to harass the British forces. In retaliation the British adopted a scorched-earth policy, burning farmhouses, driving off cattle, and carrying women, children, and the aged to concentration camps. Typhoid swept through the camps and thousands died. This last act of British barbarism some descendants of the Boers can neither forgive nor forget.

Many years later an electioneering politician, urging Boer-English cooperation, tried to impress his rural audience with the fact that the sun never set on the British Empire. An old Boer responded, "Not even God can trust the English in the dark."

There were Boers, however, who were prepared to put the past behind them, and preeminent among these was Jan Smuts. At the cost of being branded a traitor by many of his people, Smuts urged Boer-English cooperation and unity. By the Act of Union of 1910, the Transvaal, the Orange Free State, Natal, and Cape Province were consolidated into one dominion.

Although Smuts enjoyed the support of most Cape Afrikaners, and of the English in Natal, old wounds, aggravated by the new foreign — and largely English — control over commerce, continued to fester. Finally in 1948, as a direct result of the disillusionment of those who followed General Smuts into involvement in Britain's struggle for survival against Hitler, the voice of moderation was silenced and the Nationalist party was elected to power.

It is in this tragic history that the worst aspects of subsequent authoritarian Boer retribution are rooted. Many are to blame, few are free of guilt, and a lovely land suffers the threat of ruin at the hands of bitter men.

*   *   *

How could these two bowler-hatted businessmen, whose horizon was a patch of suburban grass, the cost of living, and the cricket score, talk so glibly of bloodbaths in South Africa?

It was on that morning on the 9:05 to Victoria that Mr. September came alive.

1

---

*The person under house arrest will be required to report
to the police station nearest to his registered place of
residence each day at 9 a.m. and again at 6 p.m.*
*The person under house arrest is prohibited from having
any communication, direct or indirect or through a third
party, with any other banned person.*
*The person under house arrest will not meet with more
than any two persons at any time.*
*The person under house arrest will not leave his registered
place of residence between the hours of 7 p.m. and
8 a.m.*
*Failure to comply with any of these regulations will be
punishable.*

Why am I, Paul Pendrake, born and bred white South
African and Afrikaans-speaking, deprived of the respect and
authority earned in a distinguished career? Why am I an
embarrassment to my colleagues and a threat to my family?
And the question above all questions . . .?

Well, there are just certain things that a man must do and
to hell with them!

The thoughts wrenched me from anxious sleep.

As far back as I can recall, waking has been this way for

me: variable and seldom of long duration, a singular interlude of vivid clarity between conscious coping with the charades and realities of public living and the very private meanderings of what, for want of a better word, I can only call my soul. A moment, on occasion, of total joy, when the gray longings of a dream world are suddenly vested in the warm glow of familiarity; at other times, a moment of profound relief at escape into reality from the mixed terrors of the night. Sometimes a moment when vague subconscious anxiety is starkly focused, and the cold beauty of the lonely challenge of surgery to be performed within the hour chastens the heart before the efficient sounds, smells, and bustle of the operating room submerge the episode in commonplace statistical routine. Often a moment of reluctance to face the anticipated complexities of a human day, as yet unprotected by the armor of authority, custom, or compromise. Sometimes a moment desperately cherished lest the elusive balm of truth it promises should once again slip out of reach of my nearly conscious mind.

Today my awakening was exquisitely poignant.

I turned over in bed to find my watch. It was just before six; I had two hours before it would happen . . .

How many people live in the present? For most, it's all purpose, property, prayer, and eventual pension — all future tense. The obsession with tomorrow obscures the gift of each day.

Paul Pendrake, F.R.C.S., South African. Son of an emigrant Cornishman and the daughter of a Huguenot family. Now a middle-aged surgeon, financially secure, at the peak of my career. Secure? Could my generation, children of the Great Depression of the 1930s, ever feel secure?

Another haunting thought . . . Kobie, did your great leap gain freedom for your soul? Dear Kobie, where are you this day?

For me there is only today.

12

On how many days had I undressed, slept, and dressed in this room, careless of its grace and privilege? The red mahogany of my bow-fronted Georgian chest glowing in a sunbeam, motes of dust dancing across the bright face of the cheval mirror, white beading framing tan leather wall panels, and white molded ceiling above tall sash windows, all very lovely. A house much photographed for glossy magazines; "an interior decorator's dream."

I stretched flat on my back, and folded my hands under my neck. There is a strange comfort in the ultimate loneliness of finality. A breeze stirred the curtains, filling the room with the sweet smell of stone pine and the new-mown glory of my summer garden. Never, I thought, in my twenty-five years of medical practice, had I seen acceptance of the finality of life graced by other than spiritual peace. Pray God I be granted peace this day.

Where had it all gone wrong? Compromise. Not positive, malignant compromise, but negative, soft compromise subject to the dictates of transient circumstance. Compromise in marriage, personal compromise, political compromise. Why are the lessons of the past no longer a blueprint for the future? Were the rules not written for all to read? Why should it require a martyr's death to wrest me from lifelong delusion? Kobie had been a giant of a man, wild, tough, warm, and virile. A totally free, uncompromising man. Forgive me, Jacobus September. Forgive me, God.

A rooster crowed in a neighbor's yard.

Those white voile curtains were my wife Fiona's idea; she was always careful to show her brief exposure to French culture by using the proper pronunciation of "voile." "They relieve the strong masculine tone of the room," she would say when escorting guests on a tour of the house, demonstrating her "taste" among the well-rounded people she patronized. The padded pelmets were a "professional job" executed by a bespectacled male parasite affecting a smock and a beret, who paid the colored seamstresses working for him a pittance while he pandered outrageously to the competitive affluent. Professional, antique, complete, well-rounded, textured, imported, and awful!

Was Fiona, asleep in her own suite, less lonely than I? A golden couple with a stately home in an idyllic valley, three cars, a pool, a cottage at Plettenberg Bay — he, poor darling, so frantically busy, and she such fun — crawling around like two insects of different species in the specimen bottle of marriage.

So many reasons could be postulated: the demands of work, manners, tastes, origins, or even the endless series of nameless young men in whose transient virility and social aspirations my wife found solace. Why does floundering humanity insist on confusing the symptoms with the disease? There was only one reason: I loved another woman — and I had for half a lifetime.

Before the end of this day the last strand would be severed and my soul would be totally alone. The soft, rhythmic cooing of a turtle dove in the oak outside the window was a knell. Please God, let today bring absolution.

I sprang out of bed, crossed my dressing room and twiddled the gold-plated fittings of my black marble bath to the right temperature. Stripping off my night clothes, I surveyed the man in the mirror above the basin. My hands were firm and brown, my once slim body had rounded out, but I had no belly. Despite wings of gray, I had lost none of my dark hair. My muscles were firm, and my skin had not creped, but the two deep lines from nose to mouth had extended from mouth to chin. Out of habit I did twenty-five push-ups, then bathed and dressed. Dozens of carefully pressed suits, usually the object of indecision, constituted no problem today. Selecting a loose navy shirt and slacks, I was ready to leave my home.

Passing the door of Fiona's suite, I hesitated. There was something indecent about leaving her this way. I gently eased open the door. The blinds were drawn against the

14

dawn. How long since I had entered this room? No matter. She looked unusually vulnerable curled up in the vast circular bed with its powder blue quilted valance and monogrammed handmade pillow slips. A metal clip at each temple preserved her biweekly hair styling against the neglect her sleeping pill posed. The capsule would grant her sleep until the maids brought in her breakfast at ten. It would all be over by then.

The grandfather clock whirred and struck a muted seven as I crossed the quarry-tiled hall. The door of Jeremy's room was ajar. My son was snoring thickly, his handsome young face discontented even in sleep. Education at an expensive private school, and failure to keep a series of jobs which he found "unsuitable" hallmarked his career to date, because Fiona insisted that charm, culture, and the privilege of fun were far better preparation for life than restricted academic discipline. My son was not my friend.

I left the silent house and crossed the courtyard. The early morning is a special time of day, a time reserved for birds, squirrels, and exploring dogs; a time of sweet scents, bright light, and sharp shadows before the senses are dulled and attention is dispersed. Banked blue hydrangeas against pale pink stucco walls, louvered white shutters and straight Georgian cornice below the granite rampart of the mountain behind — a truly lovely house. I took the Citroen and drove down the avenue of oaks toward the Brommers Vlei Road.

The sun rises early in the Constantine Valley. At the very moment the first ray breaches the jagged peaks of the Hottentots Holland Range to the east, the sun rushes hand-in-hand with the dawn wind across the wide waters of False Bay to flood the valley in sudden day.

How I loved this valley!

Each morning I felt gratitude that my work required me to drive into Cape Town before the eight o'clock commuters choked the roads in a snarling crush of frustration. The new highway soars over the hump of Wynberg, swoops through

15

the valley of Kirstenbosch below the wooded gash of Skeleton Gorge, then along the oak-clad slopes above the suburbs of Claremont, Newlands, and Rondebosch, the very names milestones in three hundred years of Dutch and British settlement of this loveliest of God's places.

Beyond the Groot Schuur Game Reserve, where eland and wildebeste graze in quiet disregard of the human condition, loomed the shapely pile of "my hospital." I had started my career there: it *was* my career but how it had changed! Research into creation without thought for the Creator; research to correct the catastrophic human complications of previous research. The warm humanity of individual professional responsibility surrendered to cringing accountability to bureaucracy. Change for the sake of change, an art converted to a science in a career structure reliant on statistics which could measure quantity but knew nothing of quality.

Ahead, his bare back glistening with sweat, a young Xhosa jogged up the slope in the free, distance-eating lope of his people. At the sound of my car he dove for the culvert. An illegal immigrant, lured to the city by reports of quick money that would enable him to buy the cows his tribal society demanded in return for a bride. He was late. He must have hoped to penetrate the city under cover of night. Within weeks his shining brown shoulders would be dusty gray and thin with the misery and hunger of a fugitive. If not arrested and repatriated, he would gasp out his life, the ignominious victim of savage assault in the underworld terror of the Black Townships, or at best, drag out his days in pathetic mimicry of the worst aspects of our white culture.

Round the broad sweep and over the shoulder of Devil's Peak and, as suddenly as the scene changes in a movie, I was above the most beautiful city in the world, Cape Town, nestling in the lap of Table Mountain at the very toe of Africa. Ahead of me a wraith of morning mist wrapped a scarf around the granite neck of Lion's Head. The old fishermen believed that this warned of sudden storms

16

which, within minutes, could whip the glassy surface of Table Bay into fury. But today the early sun, penetrating the yellow sulphurous smog, glanced from the mirror of the bay and twinkled on the glass faces of random office towers on the newly reclaimed foreshore.

Below Tamboers Kloof, I swung from the freeway toward District VI. As the Citroen nosed between the old warehouses, the scene that confronted me was pure Salvador Dali. In the center of a square mile of rubble, its teetering flanks shored against collapse, stood a single desolate house, evidence of the irrational lengths to which bureaucracy would go to shield nervous authority from any possible source of censure.

It would never do for the widow of a political martyr — and moreover a widow who held a foreign passport — to be ejected from her home. I smiled at my vision of the interminable solemn meetings of faceless officials debating the problem. Municipal meetings, Bureau of State Security meetings, interdepartmental meetings, cabinet meetings, until some minor official duly fortified with authority, or in error, stamped a form which condemned the widow to house arrest, while bulldozers gnawed at the very foundations of her home.

I nosed the Citroen along a track I had once known as Hanover Street. Then, pumping up the suspension, I picked my way through a maze of bulldozer tracks to the house I knew so well. A curtain stirred in the first-floor window and I knew that Carla had seen my car. My instructions were to wait.

It was 7:25 on the dashboard clock. A street sign, dangling from a leaning post, squeaked in the breeze at the corner of what had been Frazer and van der Lingen Streets. Who would recall that van der Lingen had been the first mayor of Cape Town, and Colonel Frazer a hero of Britain's early Kaffir wars? More than a century ago this district had been the most elegant suburb of a budding city. With the passage of years, new suburbs had spread along the flanks of the peninsula, and this district had become the refuge of a polyglot population of the less affluent. A place where the Cross, the Star of David, and the Crescent lived in boisterous harmony. A place of refuge for seamen looking for wine, warmth, and women, and a district which the proper Cape Town of my youth referred to as a den of most horrifying iniquity. But to those medical students who had done their midwifery training at the old Maternity Home, District VI held nothing but precious memories of a warm and uncomplicated humanity.

A shadow in the rearview mirror and I knew they were there. The back of my neck tingled with conditioned dread. Two anonymous, sunglassed faces stared immobile through the windshield of a blue police car now parked at the upper extremity of the clearing. Bureau of State Security — BOSS — God damn them!

The front door of the house banged open and Roberto backed into the sunlight, holding the door ajar with one knee as he humped two heavy suitcases. He glanced brief recognition at me, his serious face etched with anxiety beyond his years. I had always felt I knew Carla's son better than he knew me — since that fateful day in 1948 when she had carried him off the boat and presented him to Kobie as his son. I had watched him grow up and felt a special affection for him, but I never knew how Roberto regarded me. We opened the trunk of the car, without speaking, and stowed the luggage, then waited for his mother.

She stood in the doorway now — the woman I loved. Proud and passionate, the tempests of centuries of Mediterranean tumult glowing in her dark eyes. A hollowness below the high cheekbones gave a new strength to the calm of her features.

Carla would return to Rome as she wished, the proud Italian widow of an honorable man. A black shawl covered her auburn hair, accentuating the classic lines of her face, and a simple black dress almost obscured the curves of her still-youthful figure.

18

"Thank you for coming, Paulie."

I opened the car door and helped her into the seat next to mine. Roberto slid into the rear seat. He tilted a chin toward the police car. "Do not worry, Mama. They cannot harm us now."

I started the engine and steered the car through the rubble. It was not until we were through the early city traffic and swishing along the highway to the airport that I felt Carla's hand on my knee. "Remember what we have, Paulie," she said, "for the memory will always be with me, and knowing that it is also precious in your heart will ease my days and nights."

An ache in my throat muffled my voice. "You know I will, Carla."

"And be careful, Paulie. I believe this time will pass, but the passing may be dangerous for you. Perhaps some day you too can leave. There will always be a place for you in my house."

In the rearview mirror the BOSS car followed like a shadow. Controlling a mad urge to gun the Citroen to the limit and give them a run for their money, I swung off the highway toward the airport. Just beyond the turnoff, in the shadow of a culvert, three personnel carriers with riot squads armed to the teeth were waiting.

Then, as we neared the parking lot, I saw them — thousands of Cape Colored people lining the roadway in front of the terminal. Silent middle-aged men in their best suits, hats in hand, some wearing war ribbons; quiet Cape Malays, their red fezzes like poppies in a field; children in their Sunday best, frilly dresses, white shirts, and brushed hair; and bright-frocked women. I prayed that their tribute would be within the law. In the shadow of the terminal, rifles and watchful policemen with eager dogs, and beyond them an honor guard of the colored Boys' Brigade, complete with band.

I felt Carla's fingers tighten on my arm. "Sweet Mary, Mother of God, please let them be calm," she breathed.

19

I helped her from the car while Roberto showed willing porters their luggage. Carla linked her arm through mine. I felt her fingers bite into my forearm.

"We all really come from some place else, Paulie." She moved an arm to indicate all the quiet, watching faces. "Perhaps we should never have left our place, any of us." We were walking toward the familiar entrance. "Those of us who can go back, we are fortunate; so many can't. So many have no place to go. Kobie has done it: he is with God. Now I am going back to the place of my father in Rome." She lifted my hand and kissed my palm. "Paulie, perhaps you should do the same."

A Cape Colored child in a pink satin dress with bows in her hair shyly presented Carla with a vast bouquet of Protea, then gave a wobbly curtsy. "Goodbye, Mrs. September." Carla bent to kiss the child.

A news photographer scurried into range and bent on one knee to catch the moment. A policeman with a dog grabbed the bearded youth and hustled him away while he yelled something about freedom of the press.

A murmur rippled through the crowd like the little wind that precedes a storm. "Come on, move along, you there . . . move along!" The heavy voice of the policeman goaded us forward.

Then from the ranks of the Boys' Brigade, a tin whistle, beloved of the Cape Colored people, broke into "September Song." First a deep male voice and then a child's, and then the melody swelled through the crowd until it filled the sky.

I turned toward the familiar lobby.

"Goodbye, sir." Roberto's face showed no more than good manners as he shook my hand.

Carla clung to me for a long moment.

"Now we go this way," she said. The sign above the door read "Non-Whites Only." Roberto wrapped an arm around Carla's shoulders and they passed out of my life.

A dreadful sense of exclusion and deprivation of privilege engulfed me. I stood for a moment humiliated and

20

desperate. Then I sought refuge in the white section. The main concourse was deserted. I made for a distant "Restaurant" sign.

The white restaurant was almost deserted. Three business commuters, each at his own table, affected that air of resigned detachment their corporations would expect them to maintain under the circumstances. A little round man in checked trousers, seersucker jacket, and Tyrolean hat — milestones of a package tour — dejectedly poured tea for a large woman in a wig who clutched a plastic-covered fur coat to her bosom with a diamond-encrusted hand. The woman's voice was strident with anxiety.

"I've got everything with me. Did you get Hymie on the telephone? Has he got the policies? This would never have happened if we had flown straight to Johannesburg. Becky and the children will have a thousand fits. Never will I set foot on a ship again. This would never have happened if you had listened to me!"

Behind the coffee bar the proprietress grumbled in Afrikaans. "Will we never be free of these bloody coloreds?" She waved a hand at the glass cabinets. "All this stuff I ordered will have to be chucked away. All flights except this one have been canceled. How can a person live this way? Bloody Hottentots!"

I carried my coffee to a table by the window overlooking the tarmac.

2

"Look, God is saying goodnight to the house, my Kleinbaas."

Does everyone have one unforgettable moment in childhood; an experience so profound that nothing, not even the slow erosion of the years, can fog its minutest detail? Perhaps I caught a glimpse of eternity that evening.

I can see Grietjie now. Round peppercorn head, keen black eyes narrowed in concern above the high Bushman cheekbones. She stood at the great teak door, wiping her hands on her apron. Tiny bare yellow toes peeped under the hem of her blue denim smock.

When I come to think of it, relative awareness of what has been my life started at that moment — the time of the typhoid epidemic in the year of my sixth birthday. Before that day there was no definition to the kaleidoscope of large brown shiny acorns, honey and egg yolk for my croup, and the cool shuttered sanctuary of the house on hot summer days. Horseplay on the lawn and green grass scuffs on my knees, catapults which Kobie made from red rubber tubing, and the juice of white peaches dripping down my chin. Nights when I called out in terror and Kobie left the mattress where he slept in the cubbyhole off the kitchen and curled up at the foot of my bed. Days when Kobie and I wandered along the shaded banks of the Berg River, splashing in the sparkling stream, and clambering over sun-baked rock through bracken, sugar bush, and fern to reach the silent secret place where the very beginning of the river gurgled out of the granite heart of the mountain — a place that we felt was our very own. The soapy sweat smell of Uncle Gert Cillier's huge chest as he lifted me onto his shoulder. My mother, Bella, always deliciously cool and remote as the princess in the picture book in my room, and the gleam of my father's riding boots which Kobie polished for hours till you còuld see your face in them. Those were halcyon days.

On this evening of the beginning, my bed had been wheeled onto the broad stoep. Perhaps the metabolic response of convalescence intensified my sensory perceptions. Light-headed and weak as a kitten after the six weeks of the boiled-water-only treatment of my enteric fever, I lay savoring blessed relief from the delirium. Kobie sat cross-legged on the broad flagstones of the stoep, fashioning a whistle from a reed.

Even at the age of ten he was showing characteristics which set him apart. There was the promise of remarkable physique. He stood a head taller than his diminutive mother. His limbs were strong and well muscled under his tawny skin, and a warm underglow gave his cheeks an apricot flush. His hair was straight and jet black, and his nose well formed with a flair of nostril like that of his mother Grietjie. The eyes above high cheekbones were always smiling, unless he were reproved; then they developed an inscrutable flatness.

His name, duly entered on a baptismal certificate by the aging rector of the Mission Church, had been Grietjie's choice. A name like that of thousands of illegitimates of mixed blood, anonymous and inoffensive, chosen rather as a shepherd might name one of his flock by some chance characteristic of appearance, circumstance, or behavior. To Grietjie, September, the month of his birth, seemed not only appropriate but as good as any other. Jacobus, too, I suppose was sufficiently common and acceptable.

Not that his name was of much significance to her son, for like all the colored folk, he was known by his first name, and that in friendly abbreviated form. To all the world he was Kobie, and he had no reason to wish it any different.

Kobie accepted and shared his mother's vocation of total cloistered service to my family. It was a good life and Kobie was proud and happy to accept that, should anything occur which might be interpreted as being to my disadvantage, he would have to face his mother and give account. If anything disturbed the tranquillity of his heart, it was this possibility.

Perhaps the circumstance of his conception intensified Grietjie's reluctance to allow Kobie any association other than with the family. Grietjie was held in considerable awe by the rest of the colored servants whom she dragooned with distant and implacable severity. Kobie, living in the little cubbyhole off the kitchen with his mother, was forbidden any contact with the children who swarmed round the laborers' cottages by the river.

"They do not wipe their noses or wash — they will give the Kleinbaas horrible sicknesses."

Across the valley I watched the blue mountains turn gold, then salmon, fading to purple as the day died. A great tumult of cloud banked in the western sky. Then, just as the evening star gleamed, a single ray of sun pierced a cleft in the peaks, and the house gleamed golden among the darkening vineyards. The shadows of great oaks were blue daubed on the high white gables. There were flecks of cobalt in Kobie's spiky hair and his skin gleamed bronze. The very sky seemed to be holding its breath. Kobie's black eyes met mine. I lay still, afraid to move a muscle, lest anything fracture the moment.

"God is saying goodnight to the house."

The intrusion of Grietjie's voice made me sob in an agony of unaccountable despair. Seeing my tears, she hugged me to her, patting my shoulders.

24

"Come, my Kleinbaas, you are overtired. The air is turning cold. Grietjie has a nice supper for you — and if you eat nicely Grietjie will tell you a story."

She wrapped me in a shawl.

"Carry the Kleinbaas to the kitchen," she told Kobie, "and be careful. He is very weak."

Kobie rose to his feet. I recall the easy strength with which he carried me through the dark gloom of the hall, and the familiar smell of his neck as I clung to him.

Orange light flickered in the wide black range in the kitchen, dancing on copper and bright rows of bottled preserve. The air was fragrant with newly kneaded dough, spice, and cleanliness. Kobie settled me on the high chair by the table before squatting on the meal bag by the range which was his place.

Grietjie served me a brown freshly boiled egg, junket, and a slice of white toast. Then she settled herself by the table and began stripping beans.

"Come, my Basie, eat your supper and Grietjie will tell you a story."

"Please, Ma, tell us a Boer War story," Kobie begged.

It was our favorite story — dramatic, poignant, inspiring, partisan, and violent, with just enough touch of the forbidden to infuse two small boys with a delicious sense of intrigue. Forbidden because with the instinct of children we registered that Grietjie would only tell the story when she was alone with us; and because my father Jonathan and my mother Bella, the leading characters in the tale, conscientiously dismissed my questions with evasions like: "Now who would have told you about that?"

During winter vacation perhaps thirty years later, driven by the strange compulsion that prods some men to seek out and define their origins, I undertook a lonely pilgrimage to the eastern Free State. I found what had once been my grandfather Paul Malan's farm much as it must have been on that fateful night in August 1901. To the west the endless empty grassland of the Orange Free State stretched to the very rim of the earth. Except for great castles of cloud above the jagged blue peaks of the Maluti Mountains, to the east there was nothing but sunshine in the vast dome of the sky. To the north the conical mound of Spitskop, like a mammoth molehill on a vast lawn, rose unaccountably from the plain. A red gravel road skirted the hill, and beyond a small house with Flemish gables nestled in the foothills. Beyond cultivated fields of maize, a herd of red cattle grazed indolently across the veld. Disturbed by the intrusion of my car, a Basuto piccanin, his legs barely visible under his blanket, ran like a ruffled partridge toward native huts perched precariously on the rocky lip of the escarpment. Those were the huts where Letsi the Basuto must have lived. This was the place my great grandfather Malan had chosen as his sanctuary over a century ago. The place he had died to defend. The place where my Irish grandmother had died alone while my grandfather was away fighting the Boer War. The place where my mother Bella was born.

"Please, Grietjie!"

Grietjie put down her knife, hunched her shoulders, and folded her hands into her armpits, rocking to and fro.

"Well," she began, "I'll tell you how it all ended for us. It was a cold, cold winter in a terrible year. There were needles of ice in the wind as it combed through the brown grass and whistled around the house. The red cattle clumped together with their tails to the east. It is bad to be hungry, cold, and alone."

"Why were you alone?" I asked.

"For a year we were alone on the farm — the sweet Nonna your grandmother, my Kleinbaas, your mother Miss Bella, younger than you are now, and my mother Lena and I —as old as Kobie is now."

"Where was Grandpa Paul Malan?"

"Your Grandpa Paul Malan was fighting the English."

"Why was he fighting the English?"

Grietjie shrugged. "That I do not know. But we lived very happily in the Orange Free State until the English came. I heard Baas Paul say that his father had left his farm in the Cape Colony and trekked across the Orange River. Finally, after months of hardship, they settled in the Orange Free State. That is why they called it the Free State — free of the English, you see. Others felt is was not far enough and trekked further across the Vaal River. They called their place the Transvaal."

"What did the English want?"

"They wanted gold — the gold found in the Transvaal, and we, the people of the Orange Free State and the Boers in the Transvaal, did not want them among us. And the Nonna, your grandmother who was Irish, hated the English like a meerkat hates a snake. The Nonna said those devils would sell their souls for the smell of gold."

"How could they sell their souls?"

"The Nonna said that was the trouble. The English have no souls."

. "But Papa is English!"

Grietjie got her witch look.

"Shame on you, Baas Paul. Have you not seen the black spot on your father's cheek? He is one favored by the little people. They put the spot on their favored ones. If a time comes when life is too hard to bear, the little people come in the night and prick the spot with a thorn till it bleeds. Soon they take the favored one back into their care."

"But Papa was in the war."

"Many men go to wars which are not of their making. Your papa is definitely not an *English* English. And if you ask too many questions, I will tell you no more."

Grietjie poured milk into my mug.

"For a year in that war we were alone on the farm. The cattle were wild and thin. There was no sugar, no salt, and only dried meat. Sometimes Letsi the Basuto, who had his kraal on the krantz above the farm, brought us kaffir corn and firewood. He also brought news when the native drums spoke of Baas Paul Malan. It was said that Baas Paul could shoot the left eye out of an Englishman before anyone else could even see the man; and cut the wires which carried the English news, so that they ran about the veld like ants when their nest is disturbed. He could disappear into the shadows of the veld like a ghost. For with Baas Paul rode Mannetjie the Bushman who was my father. Mannetjie had given his spirit to Baas Paul as I have given mine to Miss Bella and Kobie has given his to you, my Kleinbaas."

Kobie's eyes met mine in the firelight and there were prickles down my spine.

"Why did Mannetjie give his spirit to Grandpa Paul Malan?"

"Because, my Kleinbaas, few Bushmen can otherwise live away from their people. For those of us who do stay alive, we are only the shadow of the keeper of our spirit."

Grietjie packed more wood into the range. "Then the sweet Nonna died and Letsi the Basuto put her in a box and buried her on the farm." She sniffed, twisting her little flat nose.

"Why did Grandma die?"

"She was hungry and weak; then she got sick." Grietjie wiped her hands on her apron and sighed.

"For weeks the drums told very little till one day Letsi the Basuto said that after three years of killing, the Boers were defeated, and the English were moving across the veld like locusts. They were burning farms, and taking the old people, women, and children and locking them up in barbed wire camps. But there was still hope. We heard that Baas Paul was safe and we knew he would soon come home, for Mannetjie could read the veld like a preacher reads the Book. Also Mannetjie could see in the dark."

"Was Mannetjie really my *oupa*?" Kobie's face was eager.

"Not that there is much sign of it . . . But there was fur-ther bad news. Johannes Verwyt, our neighbor, was an in-former for the English — a traitor to his people. Baas Paul had forbidden him to set foot on our farm. He was bad with colored women."

"How was he bad?"

"Bad is bad and good is good," Grietjie said. "Johannes Verwyt was bad."

"Was he the father of Dominee Piet Verwyt?"

Grietjie clapped her hand over her mouth in mock regret.

"Everyone has a father — every living soul on earth has a father — every calf, every pup has a father. Yes, my Klein-baas, Johannes Verwyt was the father of Dominee Verwyt who preaches in the Dutch Church in our village."

"Tell us about Baas Paul Malan," Kobie urged.

"Well, the English came to the house — twenty of them on horses and all dressed the same. Letsi had warned us and we hid Miss Bella under the bed because Letsi said they took only Boer children. But fie, she crawled out and spoke English to the soldiers. Then the chief of the English who was small like a Hottentot, with hair around his mouth like a hunting dog, called Johannes Verwyt from among his men. At the sight of Verwyt, Letsi the Basuto drew his assegai from under his blanket. He would have killed the traitor on the spot had not a soldier clubbed Letsi with a gun.

"Then one of the English with a black spot on his cheek took Miss Bella by the hand and gave her a cookie and laughed with her. Late in the afternoon the English rode away and we were glad."

"And then, Ma? And then?"

"That night when the moon had gone, a jackal cried to the east, and then a jackal howled to the west, and Lena my mother put a single candle in the kitchen window and shaded it three times with a dish as Letsi had said she must do. Soon Baas Paul Malan came into the kitchen. Ag, how thin he looked! His clothes torn and covered with mud, and his beard matted. He moved through the house like a mad-man, looking for the Nonna. There was no need for us to speak. He crashed his fist on the eating-room table so hard it splintered from end to end. Then he buried his face in his folded arms and wept like a child."

Grietjie heaved a deep sigh.

" 'Bring me paper and ink.' Baas Paul said. Then he wrote a letter. My mother Lena and I gave him bread and the last of the coffee but he would not eat. 'Take the food to Mannetjie,' he told Lena. 'He is with the horses by the dam. Do not take a light.' Baas Paul sat there by the table and wrote again. His face was that of a leopard at bay. I was frightened and crept to the kitchen and sat by the fire as Kobie is sitting there now."

"What then — what happened then?"

Grietjie banged the flat of her hand on the table in a gesture of despair.

"A gunshot — then another — horses — and men trampling about the house — and shouts — and I knew that Mannetjie my father and Lena my mother were dead."

There were tears in Kobie's eyes, I saw.

"Your grandpa swore a great oath, my Kleinbaas — it was a cry of rage beyond words. I crept into the shadow by the fireplace as he grabbed his gun and rushed for the door. He fired, and an English soldier fell into the kitchen — then the world exploded with gunfire and your grandpa lay dead with blood on his beard. Then from the corner I saw the traitor Verwyt among the English. Even the presence of death could not teach him manners — he had his hat on his head in our house. He would not have come in at all if Baas Paul had been alive. I heard Miss Bella cry from the bedroom, and I tried to creep around the wall to go to her. Johannes Verwyt made a grab for me." Grietjie bared her small teeth.

"I bit him!" She placed both hands on her crotch. "He screamed like a stuck pig."

"Good, Ma, good!" Kobie's eyes were wild with excitement.

"Then the Englishman with the black spot sent Johannes

Verwyt outside and took me gently, very gently, to Miss Bella."

"What then, Ma?"

"I was glad the Englishman with the black spot was there. I could see that he too was a chief among the English, and that the older chief with hair around his mouth was a lesser man. He pointed to the letter on the table, and there was an argument about Miss Bella. She crept close to me on the bed. We lay still as mice.

"Then in the morning we left in the cart, Miss Bella and I, with five English on horses. When we came round the side of Spitskop we saw the smoking shell of Johannes Verwyt's house. The English stopped. In the ashes they found Johannes Verwyt with his belly slit open, and the fat vrou dead with her face gone, and I knew that Letsi had found medicine to make his shadow grow longer."

"Why had Letsi's shadow shrunk, Ma?"

"Letsi felt he had failed in his duty to Baas Paul Malan. He loved Baas Paul. Then further in the veld we found the child of Johannes Verwyt crying like a lost baboon with the tendons of his leg cut."

"Is that why Dominee Verwyt walks funny?"

Grietjie drew a finger across the back of her right knee.

"I knew that Letsi had hoped the child would die. It was not Letsi's way to kill a child."

"And then, Ma?"

"The Englishman with the black mark took the child of Johannes Verwyt into the cart. I moved over so that the child would not come near Miss Bella, and for three days we drove across the veld to Bloemfontein. The Englishman was very kind to Miss Bella. With the letter we came to Cape Town in the train to the farm of Baas Paul Malan's sister who was the mother of Baas Gert Cilliers, and we all grew up together."

"What happened to the kind Englishman with the black spot?"

"He went back to his country. Then he fought a war

31

against the Germans who shot him in the leg. But he never forgot about us. One day when Miss Bella's heart was sore because Baas Gert Cilliers was married to the fat Miss Hannah, he came back to us. Then he bought this farm Fleur and restored the vineyards and revived the wine. Soon the Englishman and Miss Bella were married and we all lived happily ever after."

That, I thought, was the beginning of my two lives — my life with Kobie — human, real, and predictable — and my other life, inhuman, unreal, and unpredictable.

3

"You know, old chap, irrespective of race, age, color, creed, or sex, there really are only two kinds of people in the world . . ." My father lifted the cover from one of the breakfast dishes on the sideboard. ". . . those you want around you when things get rough and those you don't — it has always seemed to me that the latter are in the majority."

He turned and raised an inquiring eyebrow at me. "How is your face this morning?"

"It still smarts a bit and hurts when I chew."

He settled at the head of the long table and unfolded a napkin. It seemed to me that the black mark on his cheek looked raised and livid in the morning light.

"Kobie shaped up pretty well last night, didn't he? He saved your bacon, you know. You are fortunate to be able to chew at all. Pretty regular fellow, Kobie. Don't forget the two types. When you are older you will learn to smell the difference. You owe that young man your life."

*   *   *

And my father Jonathan Pendrake, the man with the black spot — what would he think of all this? What would he think of me now? What would he have done faced with my dilemma?

The two young men from BOSS, their cropped heads, dark glasses, and studied nonchalance ridiculously conspicuous in the tense atmosphere of the terminal, hesitated momentarily at the restaurant door. They moved to a table by the wall. Behind copies of the morning newspaper they were observing me in a mirror.

What would my father do or advise were he sitting across the table from me in this ghastly airport restaurant? My essentially Victorian father would, as I so often remember him doing, throw back his head and laugh.

"Well actually, old chap, when you really come to think of it, the whole show is a bit old hat."

Those years of my father, how short they had been! Frustrated and disillusioned by the horror of the First World War, he had left his beloved Cornwall, married my mother Bella, and devoted his future and his heart to this new land and to the making of good wine.

I can see them now — Uncle Gert Cilliers and my father, tasting the first vintage in the monastic gloom of the kelder at Fleur. They christened the wine "Belle Fleur."

Gert Cilliers, my mother's cousin, land-owning, rugby-playing, Afrikaans-speaking, descendant of French Huguenots; and my father Jonathan Pendrake, twenty years Gert's senior, a Cornish scholar, soldier, and a romantic — what was the bond between them? Love of land, love of the wine, and good faith.

Good faith — yes, that had been Kobie's strength too.

But even in my bright childhood there were shadows of what was to come. Dear Uncle Gert's fat wife Aunt Hannah refused to set foot in our house.

"She comes from the Transvaal," Grietjie said. "She hates the English."

And Uncle Gert's two sons, Willem and Petrus, visited only once and then sat apart, refusing to speak and glowering at Kobie.

And Dominee Piet Verwyt, who as a child had been rescued from the veld by my father, limping onstage to ad-

dress assembly in the Franschhoek School — I must have
been seven or eight at the time. How well I remember the
gaunt figure in the black suit, the cadaverous cheeks above a
straggly goatee.

"This day I will speak in English, but the time will come
when I shall use only my mother tongue in my own country
at all times. It is here in this very Berg River Valley that our
beloved Afrikaans language was cradled. Like a tiny seed it
has struggled for survival on rocky soil. Finally its roots will
spread into the mouths of all true Afrikaners.

"There are three types of Afrikaners — Afrikaners with
English hearts, Afrikaners with Dutch hearts, and for-
tunately, a courageous little band of Afrikaners with
Afrikaner hearts. These are the people whose hearts must be
stirred and whose help must be enlisted.

"We must learn to love our land and our people. We must
learn about our history and our national heroes. We must
revere our national feast days, and appreciate our folksongs.
This, my children, is the meaning of patriotism.

"Let us never forget that we are a chosen people! We
have a task and a mission. We must find brotherhood in our
suppression. We must love everything that is essentially our
own. Our country, our history. And above all else, our
precious Afrikaner language, which has blossomed out of
the bleeding soul of our nation. Our language is the essence
of our spiritual belonging. It must be protected and nurtured. Yes, protected, especially against attempts to
Anglicize it.

"Oh, Great Father in Heaven, bless all these Thy children
and teach them to protect, honor, and build their Afrikaans
language, casting out all others. Amen."

I recall filing back to class, filled with patriotic fervor.

I remember the garden party at Fleur on my father's fif-
tieth birthday in the year 1930. How gentle was the disposi-
tion of the Cape people, the subtle combination of tradi-
tion, grace and industry! Fleur had become a convivial
place of hospitality. A marquee on the lawn, a wine buffet

in the kelder, the long frocks of the ladies, my father in morning coat, and the scratch of my first pair of "longs." My instructions were to attend my parents, and to be introduced to society. Kobie, in new white apron, barefoot, moved among the guests serving glasses of Belle Fleur with smiling enthusiasm. He was happy that day. I well remember some of the guests as I stood in the receiving line.

Count Nicholas Rospotowski clicked his heels, kissed my mother's hand, and bowed to me. "Ah, the future master of Fleur — I have heard so many good things about your illustrious family in England."

Later at the wine buffet the Count said, "If a man has nothing and does nothing, it is a comfort to be told a new flag will put it right." The unifying influence of General Jan Christian Smuts had foundered on the economic reefs of the first great depression. The new Nationalist government was agitating for a "clean" South African flag. The tiny Union Jack in the center must go.

"Are they mad? England is our best customer!" Uncle Gert Cillier fumed, his neck muscles bulging over his collar.

"If it avoids schism, I'm all for it," my father conceded.

Count Rospotowski shrugged and wagged a long finger. "You British are beyond reason. You do not want to fight. When you fight, you win — God knows why, but you win. Then you give the loser that which you fought for. It is too amusing! But Jonathan, I do agree — the longer a dispute lasts, the more useful it is to the politician. When it is accomplished it has no value." The Count sipped his wine. "In Russia we learned what a clever rogue can persuade people to do to advance his own interests. If it is not flags, it is language, bread, race, or religion. Peasants always believe that changing masters is their salvation." He smiled ruefully. "What we never learn from history is that the new master is always worse." He put a long arm around my shoulders. "Learn, young master, learn — a peasant makes a ruthless master."

I followed as my parents moved arm-in-arm across the lawn.

"How many friends we have!" My mother squeezed my hand. "If only the whole country were like this."

"We shall see to it that it is." My father covered the hand on his arm with his own.

But later Uncle Gert got into another argument with a rather grave young man. "What is a Nationalist? He is a man who hates you — your language, your flag, your money, your guts and your children's guts — and not because he knows you or has anything against you. His language is being used to isolate him and to accentuate his feeling of inferiority so his fear may be exploited. I am a Smuts man. How can you tell me you support the Nationalists? The country is going to hell financially and they are talking flags. You must be mad!"

"The flag doesn't worry me," the man said, "nor anything else in England — if the adjustment means an end to strife, make it."

"For me the Union Jack is a symbol of order. I have not a drop of English blood in my veins." Uncle Gert's face was red. "You English will keep on judging the Nationalists by your standards and in consequence understand them even less. They hate me even more than they hate you. Why? Because I have English friends and because I see through them and I'm not prepared to gang up with my inferiors in this wretched Broederbond! I want my people to advance in open competition, not be driven into a lager of petty fear and hatred."

"Come on, Gert," my father interrupted. "Let me introduce you to a lovely young woman."

Later, when the guests had gone and I had shed my shoes and party suit, Kobie and I wandered along the riverbank in the cool September evening. The stream was in full spate after the spring rain. A random shot from my airgun flushed whirring sparrows from a thicket. A taunting Bokmakierie joined in the game, flying ahead from tree to tree, just out of range. Doves rose in flocks from the blossom-laden peach orchard. Beneath century-old oaks, the dank earth smelled warm and moldy under its blanket of fallen leaves. The stream was urgent and noisy, rolling the brown stones in its bed as if impatient to reach the distant sea. A great oak had fallen across the water, its ancient roots no longer able to support the weight of its rotting bole. Together we clambered through the spreading roots, our hands muddied. We stood for a moment, triumphant above the rushing water, our shouts echoing in the chill evening air.

"Ha, the Englishman!"

I saw them — three boys from the village, the sons of Dominee Verwyt, jeering from the far bank. "Go home, Englishman, and take your Hottentot with you."

I felt the impact of a stone against my chest; then lost my balance and toppled into the stream. The chill of the water took my breath away. The stream tugged and wrenched. My shirt billowed up around my face and the bark of the log ground into my cheek.

"Baas Paul! Baas Paul!" I heard Kobie's voice and felt the grip of his hands under my arms. He was in the water now, his legs braced against the stump and one arm around a projecting branch, hanging onto my shirt collar with grim determination. I was numb with cold.

I did not see the fading light nor the bobbing row of lanterns moving among the trees. But I do recall my father carrying Kobie's unconscious form into the nearest laborer's cottage while Uncle Gert followed with me over his shoulder.

The results of the episode were the immediate decision to pack me off to an Anglican church school in Cape Town, and the wide scar in the crook of Kobie's right arm.

*   *   *

It was 11:20 on the restaurant clock. The plane's sche-

38

duled departure was 10:30. Police with dogs were moving across the tarmac. The woman clutching the fur coat let out a long wail. "Oh, my Gawd!"

One of the young men from BOSS moved across to her. He spoke loudly.

"There is no need for panic, Missus." The woman cowered in her seat while her husband patted her hand.

"Be still, Rachel," he urged. "The authorities have the matter in hand."

Were they being kind to Carla? At least she had Roberto to support her. Everyone has someone. The crowd outside the terminal was singing again — "Die van Suid Afrika." The ponderous waves of the anthem flooded the terminal. A middle-aged businessman rose to his feet and stood at solitary attention. There was something particularly impotent in the gesture. As the last chorus died, he slumped self-consciously into his chair and blew his nose.

4

I saw my father only once after the accident. He visited me briefly at school on Founders' Day. The black mark on his cheek had been surgically removed, and somehow the well-loved face looked bereft, like a wall when a familiar picture is taken down. Within a few months the malignant melanoma had spread to his liver. The little people had carried Jonathan Pendrake to a happier place.

We sat in the study at Fleur — my mother, Uncle Gert Cilliers, Kobie and I. To me it seemed that Fleur had died. Every room mourned my father. The sun streaming through the high sashes seemed to search for him. Each book on his desk mutely craved his attention.

"He will be so pleased to be coming home." My mother stood at the window.

I saw it then — the long black hearse turning between the white pillars, and following, too numerous to count, cars crawling nose to tail.

Subdued in grief, the colored farm laborers clustered respectfully by the kelder — men in Sunday suits, women in frilly hats white and pink, and white-socked children with ribbons in frizzy hair. Six men gathered round the shiny hearse. I recognized Count Rospotowski, General Packett from Simonstown, and the chairman of the Wine Cooperative. I did not know the other three men who carried my father's coffin. The family — my mother and I, Kobie and Grietjie — followed Uncle Gert's solid back through the gate in the low white wall. Then came the people — hundreds of people following my father's coffin through the old vineyard to the newly dug grave by the bamboo grove. The wind sighed in the trees, flapping the priest's robes.

"Let us pray."

The sloping light glinted on the river. I felt my mother's hand tighten on mine. She whispered her own prayer:

"Jonathan, my precious love. How you came into my life — to flow swiftly through this valley, unmindful of the murky backwaters, oblivious to the ugly stagnations and the deep treacherous pools, impatient in the long quiet reaches but giving joy and love and life. And look what you have done, my darling — this house, these vineyards, your wine, our son. Please wait for me. There are things I have to do. Oh, my love, my precious love! Be happy. Please be patient. Please wait."

My mother clung to me. "He will be happy here, don't you think?"

Grietjie's eyes looked glazed, and her face was a mask. I thought of the little people. "Of course, Mama. Papa will be happy here."

The reading of the will. Mr. Fairweather, the lawyer, came to Fleur. Uncle Gert was co-executor.

"We must sell the place," Mr. Fairweather said. "All liquid assets in the estate have evaporated with the collapse of the shareholdings. Cape Platinum took the lot. The creditors have all filed claims."

"I had decided to leave Fleur anyway," my mother said. "You must see that I cannot live here now. There are too many ghosts. Young Paul needs me. I can get a post with the Girls' High School in Paarl. Paul can attend the Boys' School. We must be together, you see." My mother smiled. "So really there's no problem. I've already made up my mind."

41

"We must sell the property," the lawyer said.

"Never!" Uncle Gert broke in. "We will do no such thing. In this depression it will fetch nothing. No one could afford to buy Fleur and make a living. Even if they did they would ruin the vineyards and spoil the wine."

My mother tried to interrupt, but Uncle Gert would brook no argument.

"There will be no question of obligation, Bella. Like everyone else I cannot afford to buy or even hire Fleur at the moment. I will however farm it, and give you half the profits. Things may get worse or they may get better, but I'm not going to let Fleur die. It is a living wine, and a good wine. I know it, and I think it will get to know me. I will have the pleasure and half the profit." Uncle Gert smiled. "Where can I go for pleasure if I can't come here, Bella? I have two sons. Petrus will inherit my farm, Drakenhof, and Willem will inherit his mother's property in the Transvaal. In ten years Fleur may once again come into its own. We must do this for young Paul."

"Who will live in the house?" my mother asked.

"We will talk of that when the time comes. If necessary we will lock it up."

For the first time since father's death my mother's control snapped. She ran from the room.

How I hated that little house on Patriot Street in Paarl. Squat and tin-roofed, it crouched behind a dusty myrtle hedge. A ridiculously filigreed cast-iron veranda shrouded the rooms in dismal gloom even at high noon in the middle of summer. The few pieces of furniture we had brought from Fleur looked uncomfortable and somehow resentful, symbolizing my own exile.

Kobie slept in a room off the tiny yard. It had one small iron-barred window high on the back wall. Metal rings in the unplastered brick and a cobbled floor were reminders of its original purpose. How lonely he must have been! He helped Grietjie around the house, tended the exhausted little garden, and sometimes in the evening sat in on lessons when my mother took time from her work to tutor me. Grietjie forbade Kobie to associate with the coloreds in the town.

"They never wipe their noses nor wash their hands. They will give us all horrible diseases."

This restriction made his isolation total. He retired to his room when white children visited the house. On their departure he would emerge and we would be together as in the old days at Fleur.

*　　*　　*

"Beep — beep — beep —" The high-frequency note was just audible. One of the young men from BOSS extended the antenna of a pocket intercom. The other turned to look at me, his eyes blank behind his sunglasses.

What in God's name was delaying Carla's plane? Did they really expect me to make a run for it? Their heads were together now across the table. Do what you like, you silly bastards. I have nothing to lose. I am not moving out till I'm ready.

*　　*　　*

Even then the country was in the throes of political ferment. The Nationalist government refused to abandon the gold standard. At the Boys' High School you were either a NAT or a SAP. I was automatically classified as a SAP. There were daily faction fights in the playground.

"The humiliation of adapting our currency to Britain's devaluation!" Dominee Piet Verwyt wrote indignantly in *The Paarl Post*. "Why should Afrikaners be subjected to this ignominy after all the years of bitter struggle to free ourselves from the English yoke? The Afrikaner will be trodden underfoot by the Hochenheimers. He will be a slave in his own country. How is the Afrikaner going to benefit from

43

devaluation when he has nothing? The railway worker, the mine worker, the patient thousands of penniless Afrikaners on relief schemes — their pay packet will only be worthless."

Uncle Gert discovered a secret Broederbond circular addressed to his elder son at Drakenhof. He stormed about our little house and flung the pamphlet on the dining room table. I picked it up and read:

"Brothers, our main consideration must be whether Afrikanerdom will reach its ultimate destiny of domination in South Africa. Brothers, our objective is not whether one or another party will obtain the whip hand, but that the Afrikaner Broederbond shall govern South Africa."

Meanwhile the people starved and millions of pounds left the country. Broederbond propaganda persuaded the faithful that Britain, and Britain alone, was responsible for their plight. In their distress the people clung as never before to the Dutch Reformed Church, and to Dominee Verwyt.

It was one of those still, baking December nights in Paarl when the breath of the valley is heavy with the scent of fig trees, watered lawns, and pine resin. The little house on Patriot Street was like an oven. My mother was giving extra lessons at school.

"Let's go out," Captain Justice said. "Just for a walk."

He was a tall boy, Alan Just — seventeen years old, and son of the Anglican clergyman. His hook nose, lanky frame, and the affectation of a yachtsman's cap, which only left his head in class, had earned him the distinction of being nicknamed after a contemporary fictional hero.

"Did you ask Miss Bella?" Kobie asked as we passed through the yard.

"We won't be long," Captain Justice said.

"Baas Paul does not go out without Miss Bella's permission."

44

I followed Captain Justice.

"Then I am coming too," Kobie said, pulling on a shirt and coming out into the moonlight.

Down Patriot Street and along the Berg River we strolled, Kobie keeping ten paces in the rear. We came to the colored quarters bordering on Lady Grey Street. There were shouts of abuse as a woman armed with a broom chased a lurching man from a house. The man's face was bleeding. The roadway was muddied and littered. Across the street in a darkened house, a gramophone wheezed and people clapped their hands to the beat of the music. The sordidness had a strange fascination. Ahead under a streetlamp a crowd watched a game of klawerjas on the pavement. We edged between the onlookers. One of the youths seemed to know Kobie.

"*Aitsa*, Kobie! So at last you have left the white people to have some fun. Come and sit next to me and play."

"No thanks," Kobie smiled. "I will just watch."

The youth turned to a girl in the crowd.

"You see, Chrissie, the white people don't even give him any money."

The girl with fuzzy hair smiled a pitying little smile.

"Finished!" The big youth clapped his hands and collected coins spread on a grubby rag on the pavement. "You klonkies will have to grow up before you play with Stoffel!"

There was laughter, grumbling, and cursing. The game was over.

"How much have you got?" Stoffel addressed Captain Justice.

"Five shillings."

"What about him?" Stoffel tilted a chin at Kobie.

"He's alright," Captain Justice said.

"Wait here!" Stoffel said. He pocketed the five shillings and disappeared into an alley.

"What's he going to do?" I asked the Captain.

"Wait and see the fun! I come here often."

45

Chrissie was leaning on Kobie's shoulder while she removed a pebble from her canvas shoe. She hummed to herself in the darkness. Her hair smelled of coconut oil.

Stoffel came back a few minutes later. "I've got it!" he said.

What was "it"? I wondered.

On we walked, Stoffel leading the way, Chrissie arm in arm with Kobie, over the railway along the river, and under the great black hulk of the iron road bridge.

"Here we are!" Stoffel squatted down and struck a match. He moved flat stones to reveal two small holes a foot apart in the clay. He squatted on the foundation of a pylon and held up a small brown parcel.

"This will take us all to heaven." He winked at me. "Bring some water," he told Chrissie.

The girl walked to the river, cupped her hands and ran back to pour water into the hole in the mud.

"More," Stoffel said, "much more. Help her, Kobie."

"Have you smoked dagga before?" Captain Justice asked me.

"You must be joking!"

"Not at all. If you don't want to it's up to you. I often come for a whiff. Marvelous stuff!"

"But it's against the law!"

"So what?"

Stoffel put some of the bag's contents into the empty hole and lit it. There was an aromatic smell under the bridge. He partially covered the smolder with a flat stone. Lying on his stomach, he put a reed to his mouth. Chrissie lay face down over the other hole. Smoky bubbles burst through the water with a flat plop. She breathed them down eagerly, humming under her breath. She moved away to lean her head on Kobie's shoulder. Then Captain Justice inhaled a little smoke.

"Now you," Stoffel told Kobie.

"You — now you!" Chrissie led him forward. "I will blow for you."

The Captain giggled. "I feel wonderful."

Chrissie moved slowly. She lay on her face, blowing on the reed. The lights of a car passing over the bridge glinted copper on her thighs as she lay with legs spread.

Kobie was breathing the smoke in deeply — again, and again, and again.

"That's enough," Stoffel hissed. "Don't be so greedy."

He was sitting by the pylon, rocking back and forth, his head in his hands. I wanted to leave, to run out of this ghastly nightmare.

"Kobie," I said, "we are going home!"

Kobie's eyes looked mad. He threw back his head and laughed in my face.

"No, you don't!" Captain Justice gripped my arm. "You're not going anywhere till I say so!"

Chrissie moved to where Kobie sat on the pylon. She was lurching slightly. She put an arm round his neck, smiled into his face, and swung her thigh across his knee. I saw that she was naked under her short cotton dress. Kobie growled like an aminal. He swung her onto her back. Her white canvas shoes waved in the air before locking round his waist. A passing car drowned her moans as they jerked together under the bridge.

The Captains' hand bit into my arm. "She's a wildcat, that one," he said between his teeth.

I was sweating with horror. The whole structure of my life had come unstuck. What would my mother and uncle Gert say?

"We will go now," the Captain said after a while. He still gripped my arm. Stoffel, I noted, had disappeared.

We climbed up the bank, through the bushes, out onto the road. Chrissie was giggling slightly. Kobie's arm was around her waist. They stopped for a moment at the corner of the street where Chrissie lived to peer into the lighted window of Pinn's Bargain Store.

"I would like a brooch like that one." Chrissie pointed to a display of gaudy trinkets.

Kobie looked around. Then he bent and lifted the iron grill from a storm drain. With the strength of ten, he flung it through the plate glass.

"I'm off!" Captain Justice ran into the darkness.

Kobie was leaning through the shattered glass. He stood back roaring with mad laughter, waving a hand full of junk.

Then I, too, ran. I heard my mother return minutes after I had dived into bed.

Grietjie's face was blank when the police called the next day. "Yes," she said, "he is my son. I have no knowledge of this. I know nothing more. I am sorry."

My mother was horrified. "There must be some mistake. We love him. It simply cannot be true! Not Kobie!"

"I'm sorry, madam. It took five of us to hold him down. There is no doubt." I watched the policeman stomp down the path. How could I add to my mother's distress? Would confessing help Kobie?

How that night haunted me! I spent weeks of fear, doubt, and horror. Alan Just still wore his peaked cap with élan. At school I avoided him conscientiously, going through endless lengths of indignity. He did not come to our house on Patriot Street again.

Three weeks later the case was reported in *The Paarl Post:* "Jacobus September, colored, aged sixteen, convicted of housebreaking with intent to steal, and on a second charge of being under the influence of dagga. On the first charge the accused was sentenced to five years in reform school and on the second to ten cuts with the cane." Kobie refused to testify.

"I've been to see him three times," Uncle Gert said. "There is more to this than meets the eye. He thanks me for coming and means it. Then he won't talk. Well, if he has really been mixed up with rubbish, he is better off where he is."

"Is there anything he needs?" my mother asked.

"Yes, he wants his mouth organ. Do you know where it might be, Paul?"

As for me, I said nothing.

Do people really change with circumstance? Throughout, Kobie's response to life's changing pattern had been consistent; and so, when I come to think of it, had been mine.

That was the first time I denied him.

5

Those floundering years of my adolescence before Hitler's war . . . what bitter years they were! Desperately lonely, tortured by insecurity and doubt, I became deeply resentful of the consequences of our reduced circumstances. I equated all humanity, except my mother, Uncle Gert, and Grietjie, with the hideousness under the bridge.

"Get an education, my boy, that is the one thing they can never take away from you."

Goaded by an irrational conviction that in so doing I could in some way atone for Kobie's plight, I flung myself into my studies with grim resolve. Even the rugby I loved, I played with a solemn determination to excel. That was how I first met Stompie Lategan. Rugby was Stompie's life. Short and blond, just five foot six, he moved his heavily muscled frame with lightning agility behind the scrum. He captained the school team with popular and successful enthusiasm.

Perhaps in those post-depression thirties we were all too busy to notice the lurking shadows of impending catastrophe. Economics finally prevailed over sentiment. A coalition government with General Smuts as deputy premier abandoned the gold standard without loss of face to the Nationalists. Slowly, money flowed back and hope brightened the bleak despair of soup queues.

But the shadows were there even then. After a brief scuffle, "Die Stem" replaced "God Save the King" as our national anthem. A short while later it was proclaimed that the Union Jack would no longer be hoisted officially with the South African flag.

Throughout the country, among his own people, Dominee Piet Verwyt was acclaimed for his unswerving Afrikaner patriotism. He was at the forefront of affairs. He was quoted in the newspapers.

But his greatest contribution was the idea of the Great Trek centenary celebration. It was made clear that this was a peculiarly Afrikaans celebration — no matter that the Afrikaans language was nonexistent in 1834. From each of the four provinces of South Africa a symbolic ox wagon trekked north through the land, converging on Pretoria. There, on December 16, the anniversary of the day that the early trekkers had defeated the Zulu chief Dingaan at Blood River, the foundation stone of a memorial to the trekkers was laid. As the wagons rolled from village to village, local Broederbond cells ensured the awakening of the South Afrikaner volk. Men, young and old, grew beards, and the women, like Uncle Gert's wife Hannah, adopted the long, high-bodiced frocks of the previous century. Oxen were roasted over open fires, and games thought to be traditional were played.

Such was the national fervor that a semi-military patriotic organization, the Ossewa Brendwag, was formed. The salute was a fist clenched over the heard. Dominee Piet Verwyt was appointed chaplain to this elite stormtrooper wing of the Broederbond. The Dominee also gave his blessing to a purely Afrikaans Chamber of Commerce, to salvage and sponsor purely Afrikaans commercial expansion and to get business out of the clutches of the English and the Jews.

Uncle Gert Cilliers took all this very seriously, but my mother laughed. "Poor Piet! He is doing his job as best he knows how. That leg of his gives him a lot of pain."

Those were the years when Hitler's unintelligible tirades came over our Philco shortwave radio, and in the cinemas the goose-stepping Nazis were a rather repetitive source of amusement. The pogroms — well, they were probably grossly exaggerated, and so very far away.

They were not entirely unsatisfactory years for me. The opportunity to spend my Saturdays assisting old Dr. van Skalkwyk at his Colored surgery gave me a source of direction. Dispensing medicine and bandaging limbs in the crowded surgery, I felt wanted and useful and privileged to be able to help those less fortunate than myself. I began to think about a career in medicine. "You have the hands and the heart," the old doctor said. "If you have the head you will make a good doctor."

The year 1939 marked the end of our youth. Hitler invaded Poland. South Africa was in turmoil, son against father, brother against brother. In the face of intense Nationalist opposition, General Smuts called for volunteers to aid Britain in her stand against Hitler.

Dominee Piet Verwyt labeled Jan Christian Smuts a traitorous English lackey, and exhorted all true Afrikaners to oppose the war effort. He gave his blessing to young Nationalist thugs who beat up isolated soldiers in city streets and canonized saboteurs when General Smuts interned them.

I was just nineteen when Stompie Lategan and I volunteered for service abroad. Somehow our war was "clean." We believed in our war. In retrospect those years were probably my happiest. Why? God knows why; but they were.

52

6

The steady wind which blew incessantly through the gray sandy waste of Helwan Camp rattled the rickety hessian-covered window of the hut, bringing down showers of the all-penetrating dust. Like the slinking Egyptian fellaheen who wafted through the camp like shadows, the wind came from everywhere, disappearing into the desert waste, leaving only the reek of the decadence of ages.

Major van Tonder studied the list of petty offenders on the desk in front of him. "Tell the Sergeant Major to bring in the first one."

The Sergeant Major threw back his head and bellowed, "September, J." The name, I recall, meant nothing to me.

"Christ, my head!" the Major groaned.

The war was Major Andries van Tonder's life. He had joined the permanent force after campaigning with General Smuts in East Africa in 1918. He was one of the many seasoned soldiers attached to hastily commissioned volunteer units in an attempt to make up for their inexperience. Malaria in the recent Somaliland campaign had fined down his already spare frame. His brown leathery skin was stretched tight over high cheekbones, and his head was shaved, revealing scars on his scalp. In the heat of the hut he smelled of gun oil, polish, blue soap, and whiskey.

I read the charge sheet: assault with intent to murder and resisting arrest by Cairo police. Civil authorities in Cairo demanded a report in the finding and an apology at the highest level. One Cairo policeman had a broken jaw, according to the report, another had a fractured arm, and a third had allegedly been kicked in the crotch. Claims for compensation would be filed.

The blinding glare and the wind rushed into the hut together as the door opened to admit the offender.

It was Kobie! At least six foot six, fatigue trousers tight over massive thighs, powerful muscles swelling bare forearms, the broad parchment-like scar on his right arm standing out gray against the copper skin. He looked at me keenly. It was a straight, uncomplicated look of recognition.

"What have you got to say for yourself?" Major van Tonder asked. "This is a serious charge."

Kobie looked directly at the major — the same flat look that came into Grietjie's eyes at times. "At precisely fifteen hundred hours, sir, I was sitting in a Cairo tram . . ."

"Don't lie to me!" The Major's voice was menacing. "How the hell did you know the time sitting on a tram?"

Kobie bent a massive left arm and indicated his watch. "My arm was leaning on the rail, sir, when this Egyptian skolly runs alongside and hooks his finger in the strap, Major. The Major must never ride on a Cairo tram. They steal everything, even false teeth . . ."

"Go on," the Major said wearily.

"So I catch him, the Egyptian skolly, by the neck, and I lift him into the tram. He screamed like a stuck pig, Major. The tram stops. The skolly pulls a knife and I bang his head against the floor. Then I am angry, Major, and I throw him back into the street. Then everyone was shouting and the police came. The captain of the Gippo police kicks the man in the street and rolls him over. He is dead, the policeman says."

54

"That is good," the Major said. "If the bastard were alive, we would have to pay a lot of compensation. Life is the only cheap thing in Cairo. Continue."

"Then the police want to arrest me. I am not going to be arrested by any Egyptian. I resisted arrest until our own MP's came to take me away. No Egyptian is going to touch me."

"You admit the charge?" van Tonder asked. "The charge is a serious one . . . confined to barracks for a week and two hours' pack drill each day. Have you anything to say?"

Kobie smiled. It was the smile of Grietjie's son.

"Yes, Major," he said. "I want to be Baas Paul's driver."

"You want to what?"

"He wants to be my driver, sir," I said.

"Do you know this man?"

"Yes, sir. He grew up on our farm. His mother Grietjie has been with my mother all her life. They are good people."

"Do you want him?" van Tonder asked. "He looks a tough bastard."

"Yes I do, sir. As a matter of fact I need him right now."

Van Tonder considered for a moment. "Write a suitable letter to the Egyptian authorities, and have it stamped by Brigade. Your sentence is suspended on good behavior."

"Thank you, sir!" Kobie's smile seemed to bring the glory of the Franschhoek Valley into the waste of Helwan Camp.

What a night that was in Cairo! The very memory of its spontaneous normality somehow makes this nightmare in the airport seem ridiculous.

Perhaps the essence of friendship is an immunity against circumstance, distance, or the passage of time. That was how it was for Kobie.

"Never complain and never explain," my father once said. Kobie did neither. The next few weeks did, however, reveal that good behavior had earned him a two-year remission of his sentence to the Special Service Battalion, a tough Foreign Legion type of unit created to relieve prewar unemployment. At the outbreak of war he had volunteered for service abroad. He was one of the thousands of Cape Colored men who, despite Dominee Piet Verwyt's successful objection to the enlistment of non-whites, were prepared to serve as unarmed drivers, batmen, storemen, and cooks in the armed struggle against Hitler.

Kobie adopted Stompie Lategan, caring for his needs as he cared for mine. Even in those days Stompie had problems. His family was bitterly divided on the war issue. The long uncertain weeks waiting for orders to move into the Western Desert seemed to change his normally good-natured efficiency into an irritable, compulsive drive. Strangely, Kobie's arrival seemed to calm Stompie.

Kobie drove our staff car into Cairo that night. Biblical figures in flowing black robes, earthenware pitchers balanced on their heads, walked sedately among the palms. A child squatted to relieve herself in a canal. On the Nile stately dhows were silhouetted against the glowing west. The slight humidity of the autumn heat seemed to accentuate the sweet, rank smells of the Cairo streets. Horse drawn gharris and antediluvian taxis moved everywhere. The continual pooping of old-fashioned bulb horns, the random movement of little blue blackout lamps, and the incessant shouting of the drivers filled the moonlit streets with diverting clamor. Dozens of urchins swarmed out of the darkness like flies as we drew up outside the Officers' Club.

"French postcards! Feelthy postcards! Pure white virgin, only fourteen years, very clean, very hygiene! Cheap! Cheap!"

Mohammed, the red-fezzed eunuch, swooped down the steps. His walleye rolling, he beat off the urchins with his staff.

"Ah, the Major, the Captain!"

Mohammed's attempt to open our car door was thwarted by Kobie's bulk. Mohammed glowered malevolently at

Kobie and bowed low. "The major has a very big servant."
My ten-piaster note disappeared into the folds of his robe
without discernible movement of his hands.

The club was empty except for three pink-trousered
Hussars.

"This is hell," Stompie grumbled. "It depresses me." He
waved to the bartender. "Give me a double scotch."

"Hello, hello, hello!" Andy Gifford burst into the bar.
We had not seen him since our rugby match against Stellenbosch University. He stood with arms wide. He had grown a
straggly blond moustache, and his crumpled tunic sported a
fresh D.F.C. and Bar. He was posted missing shortly after
that evening, but I shall remember him this way.

"Drinks all around, drinks all around. I'm a father!"
Andy fumbled in his tunic and brought out a letter. "There
it is in black and white. A girl, a beautiful heavenly girl!
Have you chaps got any kids?"

We shook our heads. He gulped a scotch. "Well" — he
was very grave now — "be warned. I've come to the conclu-
sion that the only stage of reproduction that is bearable is
the first. Terrible strain having kids. Look at me. I've enjoyed the show so far but now, believe me, I'm terrified
some bloody Hun will shoot me down and I won't see my
daughter. Another scotch, Alfred, I'm suffering from reac-
tion." He gabbled on. "The letter says my daughter has blue
eyes like mine." He folded his letter carefully and buttoned
it into his tunic pocket. "Pretty good, eh? Is there any grub
left?"

"Dinner's off," the barman said flatly.

"I'll fade if I don't eat. I'm awash. Tell you what. We'll
go to Mary's. You been there?"

"Not yet."

"Most wonderful brothel in Cairo — finest food, a band,
and a bar." Andy looked around the club, wrinkling his
nose. "My daughter would cry to see her father in a dump
like this."

"Let's go," said Stompie.

Kobie drove the staff car out to Helmieh. A crescent moon, reflected in the black water of a canal, seemed to keep pace with the car. The air beyond the city was cool and fragrant. Set among tall palms, Mary's house for officers shone silver in the desert moonlight. As we crowded through the blackout curtain there was a slight scuffle at the door as the Lebanese doorman tried to exclude Kobie. A British colonel with a stoop and a small moustache came up. He lifted an eyebrow and addressed Stompie.

"Is this man with you?"

I turned to see Kobie standing to monumental attention just inside the blackout curtain.

"It is better that I am here, Baas Paul," he said softly. "I will come no further than the door."

The Lebanese doorman was waving his arms and spluttering in Arabic.

"This man is with us," Stompie said. "He will come no further than the door. He goes where we go. Have you any further objection, sir?"

I could see the British colonel weighing his own position.

"Damned irregular, actually," he said, as he sloped off.

"My God!" Stompie grabbed my arm and pointed across the room. "There's old Wire-guts van Tonder."

A Polish officer was tinkling at the grand piano. Major van Tonder, his face a mask, stood by the bar, solemnly tapping his baton to the beat of the music.

"Beeg strong Sous Efrican!" The girl approaching our group was lovely — tall, with thick blond hair plaited and piled above a classic face.

"This is Eke," Andy Gifford said. "She's a honey."

"The food, eh?" Stompie laughed.

"Don't be suspicious. Remember, I'm a father."

"No offense — no offense."

We followed Eke across the restaurant. Even the ubiquitous uniforms could not detract from the luxurious atmosphere. The air smelled of good food and expensive perfume; the decor was colorful and exotic. A dozen or more elegantly gowned women chatted idly among the tables.

Stompie Lategan settled himself in a chair. His eyes were bright as he surveyed the room. "Why has nobody told me about this before?"

Another woman came up now. "This is Fifi," Eke said. "Now we are all together. It is just like home — not so? It is not good to be away from home. I think of my father and my sweet mother. We were in Poland when the Germans came." She dropped her eyes. "It is too tragic; it is not good to think of such things."

She lifted a chain of gardenias from the tray of a passing waiter and draped them around my shoulders. The touch of her hands on my neck sent an electric shock spreading down my spine and into my thighs.

"Have you ordered dinner, darlings? The kidneys are fresh, and the beef is English — very good."

"May I sit down and have a drink?" Fifi asked Andy Gifford.

"Oh, but please do." Andy made room at the table.

She proceeded to tell Andy her life story. "My father was an aristocrat. Our villa overlooked the Adriatic. War is so cruel; it was all too terribly sad." She sighed and looked crushed. I felt her hand caressing my knee under the table.

"How long before you move into the desert?" she asked me suddenly.

"Our army is being disbanded," Andy said, winking at me. "We're all coming to move in here with you."

"How very nice for you!" Fifi's eyes were those of a cat.

"Who is that girl over there?" Stompie asked. "What's her name?"

Following his gaze, I turned to see a girl standing alone at the foot of the stair. She wore a flame-colored sheath. Her shoulders were brown and smooth. Her dark almond eyes were insolent; white teeth shone between moist scarlet lips. Her beauty reminded me of the Cape Colored women at home.

"Find out for yourself! I'm wasting my time."

Fifi flounced off. But we watched her strut up to the girl at the foot of the stair and jerk her head in the direction of our table. The flame-colored girl looked languidly across the room. Unwinding herself like a cat, she threaded her way toward us.

"It's hell being a father," Andy Gifford murmured.

Eke was rubbing her thigh against my knee. "It is not possible to fight without love," she was saying. "We all do our part to kill Germans." She drew her slender finger across her throat and gave a gurgling laugh.

The mixed grill was excellent. The whiskey was good, although watered and ten times the normal price. Across the room Major van Tonder sat alone behind his drink.

"The Major comes here every night," Eke said. "All the girls here have tried to make him happy. He must have had a very sad life." She shrugged. "He is for whiskey, not women."

I recall experiencing a mad desire to roar with laughter. The dark girl was sitting on Stompie's lap. Her black hair was drawn into a tight knot on the nape of her neck. She was kissing Stompie on the mouth. He led her onto the dance floor. Her limbs in the scarlet sheath blended with his as they danced. Her bare arms were brown against his blond hair. The whole room seemed to sway slightly to the music. Men with women on their arms came and went on the broad staircase. I watched Stompie and the girl move arm in arm toward the stairs.

Eke was whispering in my ear. "I have a technique — how do you say in English — the ultimate?"

There was a sudden milling near the stair. Kobie was standing with arms folded at the foot of the balustrade. The stooping British colonel was there too. I shook Eke off and headed across the room. I felt, more than saw, Major van Tonder threading between the tables.

"No, Baas Stompie," Kobie was saying, "these women are all sick. They are all whores. They are worse than the worst *meide* at home."

Stompie was glaring at Kobie — desire, frustration, and common sense contending with the whiskey in his brain.

The flame-colored girl on Stompie's arm reached up and draped herself on Kobie's broad chest. She turned to address the room, head tilted back, and her moist mouth wide. "This is the biggest man in the world, and I have him all to myself."

I saw Kobie shake the woman off. The Lebanese doorman was tugging at his sleeve.

"Get the military police," the British colonel said. "One never knows where one is with colonials."

I felt a surge of anger. "South Africa is no one's colony!"

"That is bloody well right," said Major van Tonder. "What is your problem, colonel?"

A burly, kilted Scot stormed up. Under a thatch of curly black hair, he glowered like an Aberdeen ox.

Suddenly, the whole wretched boredom of Egypt seemed to erupt in the room. Andy Gifford grabbed a soda siphon and directed a jet under the Scot's kilt, and a blow aimed at Major van Tonder went wild. The Highlander yelled in fury, spun round, and buckled over Kobie's bent knee. The Lebanese crawled under a table. Stompie was surrounded and punching steadily. I clubbed an Egyptian with a chair. A bottle whistled close to my head. The British colonel went down. I turned to see Major van Tonder grinning like a monkey, taking careful aim with a bottle of Vat 69. Women, shrieking above the furor, were scampering up the stairs. Kobie picked up a table and flung it at Stompie's assailants. There was a crash, a struggling mass of limbs, and a momentary lull.

"Come on, Baas Paul, Baas Stompie, Major!" Kobie yelled.

The four of us ran through the blackout curtain and into the moonlight. Kobie drove fast along the canal road.

By dawn the First South African Brigade was moving out to the Western Desert.

7

Even now my hands sweat when I recall those early Western Desert days. For months we had been strafed, bombed, and harried. Twice a day, always twice a day, the Stukas came and the hammering scream of their sirens made strong men run shrieking into the desert. Somehow, without air support, we survived. We moved forward, were bombed unmercifully, and moved forward again, ever deeper into the windswept waste of that stony Libyan desert.

"Reconnaissance reports a force of German armor here." The C.O. pointed to a spot in the map spread out on the hood of a staff jeep.

"How many, sir?" Stompie asked.

"No details." The C.O. referred to the dispatch. "Just a considerable force of Tigers. Your battery is on the perimeter. Look to morale. The men are getting jumpy."

Back at the guns, Stompie studied his charts. Kobie served us the inevitable bully beef, biscuits and apricot jam.

"We'll sleep when the guns are set," Stompie said. "Perhaps if there is time, you could distribute that batch of Christmas mail."

A parcel had come for Stompie. It was large. "It's from my mother," he said in obvious delight. Eagerly he tore at the wrapping. Brown paper, then white paper, then newspaper. "She never had any confidence in the post," he smiled. Whatever it was, it was small now. He read the white label on the little oval tin.

The look on his face was terrible. Wrenching open the door he flung the tin far into the desert. I saw the white label gyrate in the wind. Stompie stumbled off toward the guns. I retrieved the label and read:

"Blue butter for Jannie Smuts' English lice. Moeder."

My heart contracted in rage and sorrow. What force was this that had no feeling, no mercy, no scruple? At that moment the truth dawned on me. It was fear — pure, blind, conditioned fear. Fear in the heart of this wretched woman, fear in the heart of Uncle Gert's wife Hannah, fear in the heart of Dominee Verwyt. Fear that there was no place for them beyond the thorny rampart of hate they chose to build around themselves. God damn her! Curse her and all her kind!

I heard a wild yell. Kobie stood pointing into the sun. In the clamor of warning sirens, I ran for the slit trench. The Bofors opened up. Then I saw them — half a hundred evil black Stukas and supporting Messerschmitts. Men were running everywhere, diving into slit trenches. I ground my body deeper into the hostile soil and fired my tommy gun at random. Suddenly it was all over.

A truck burned close by, the thick black smoke stinking of oil and rubber. In the distance more smoke billowed. Stretcher bearers were collecting the wounded.

Then a low whining sibilant swish. Our staff car buckled, rolled over, and burst into flames. My jangled reflexes took control, and hurled me headlong to the ground.

"Tanks, Baas Paul, tanks," Kobie yelled. He was pulling kit out of our blazing vehicle. The Tigers moved heavily through the desert, their black gauntness vicious and menacing. A tank lurched as its gun fired. The shell whispered close. I ran for the guns. The squat boom of the twenty-five pounders sounded safe and secure. Stompie was there, his blond hair wild in the wind.

63

"Fire!" he yelled. A tank fifty yards away spun crazily as the heavy shell buckled its tracks. We were firing over open sights. The low whining shells seemed to come from everywhere. Our guns fired and fired again. A shell exploded on the gun carriage.

"Fetch ammo," Stompie bellowed through the dust. I obeyed mechanically. Four gunners lay dead beside the gun. Only Stompie, Kobie and I remained. The casing was splattered with blood. Kobie was acting as loader.

"Fire!" Stompie yelled.

The tank came from nowhere. I saw the young German flourishing a Luger, and shouting from the turret. Stompie lay ten yards away. He had raised himself on one elbow. The German boy's teeth were bared. He aimed his Luger and fired. The bullets whined wide, but a shot at Stompie's prone form went home, jerking him like an invisible string. The tank lurched on.

"Baas Paul, Baas Stompie!" Kobie's voice was the snarl of a lion. With one superhuman bound he landed on the monster's unprotected back. The gibbering German boy turned too late. With one hand Kobie jerked him into the air, swung him, and beat his brains out on the turret. Then, grabbing the Luger, he fired down the open hatch. I saw him kick the dead German off the iron hulk. The tank ground to a stop.

I was rooted to the ground. Kobie rushed madly toward me. "Look out, Baas Paul, Baas Paul, Pasop!" He drove me to the ground in a massive dive tackle as the tank blew up.

I have no idea how long I lay there in the desert. I only know that suddenly it was miraculously quiet and that Kobie was wiping my face with a wet rag.

We had driven the Tigers off. Stompie had only flesh wounds and was fine. When it was dark, the First South African Brigade licked its wounds and moved off through the eternal desert wind.

8

This must be hell for Carla! Was it possible after all these ghastly months that they could, even at this critical eleventh hour, conjure up further bureaucratic obstacles to her departure? Of course it was possible. Anything was possible! I had not seen the Italian consul at the airport. Perhaps diplomatic privilege had gained him admission to the non-white section. The crowd outside the terminal was no longer singing. The staccato bark of a police dog cut through the tension in the restaurant. The squad on the tarmac nervously changed their grip on their riot weapons.

Perhaps I could catch a glimpse of Carla from the main concourse. Maybe we could even talk across a barrier or through a grille. The young men from BOSS tensed visibly as I rose from the table. As I passed the woman with the fur coat she lifted piteous eyes. "Don't leave us now, please!"

"I'm not really leaving; I shall not be long."

Her husband put a protective arm around her shoulder. "The gentleman is going to the toilet, Rachel."

The deodorized clinical whiteness of the washroom was a blessed relief. Everything is relative, I thought. I splashed cold water on my face. In the mirror I saw one of the young men from BOSS. He was standing just inside the door. I smiled at him in the mirror. Except for a downward twitch of the corners of his mouth, his face was immobile behind his sunglasses. He came across the floor, turned on a tap and washed his hands, watching me in the mirror as I used the urinal. I left him to the charade of drying his hands, and made for the main concourse. Each click of my heels on the floor echoed through the empty hall.

Except for four riot police posted at each corner, the place was deserted. I lit a cigarette. The empty rows of chrome and plastic seats looked desolate. A police dog pricked its ears and bristled as I started toward the exit. It was sealed off. I sat down on a bench overlooking the tarmac. An air hostess was coming down the stair in the tail of the waiting 727. She leaned over the rail to speak to one of the riot squad before scampering back into the plane. The murmur of the crowd outside the terminal swelled and receded like the sough of the sea.

*   *   *

Years later Carla said to me: "You were falling in love with me, Paulie. I had to work. The children had to be fed. It was not possible to work the streets if I let myself love you. What would a gentleman think of a girl like me? It was the only way, and in the end I was right, Paulie."

How right she was!

That was Rome in the spring of 1945. The war in Europe was almost over. The city teemed with troops on leave. Young people laughed and shouted in the streets, and black-frocked priests emerged from the Vatican. They were everywhere, striding about the streets with an air of urgent purpose like ants restoring their damaged colony. Children darted through the classic grandeur of the city, begging and foraging. For the Romans the war was over. The past was a blueprint for the future. It had happened before; it would happen again. The city was eternal.

Kobie had found me a furnished flat in an ancient villa.

The balcony overlooked a mosaic of city roofs, and beyond there was a glimpse of the river. My door opened onto a cloistered courtyard where a stone cherub threw a jet of water into the rippling basin of a battered fountain. Under threat of direst consequence, Kobie gave the landlady strict instructions to stay out of my room. He would attend to all my domestic needs.

Those were strange days. Relief from the rigors of combat was now uncomfortably tinged with an awareness that soon, with the end of hostilities, the rare privilege of living in the present would be lost. With the coming of peace the basic camaraderie of survival must give way to the sterility of solitary economic pursuit. Like children whistling in the dark, we were seized with a compulsive gaiety.

How different Carla was! I had been to the opera with a friend, I recall. Later I sat alone in the Via Veneto, watching the passing parade.

"May I sit with you?" The query was more formal than solicitous. Her navy blue chiffon frock was full-skirted above neat, plain shoes. The pageboy cut of thick auburn hair swung gently as she tossed her head. She wore no rouge, no obvious lipstick, no jewellery. The skin of her brown arms was satin smooth. Almond eyes, slightly prominent and wide-set, were frank but sensitive with a glint of subdued pride. Her hands were strong, tapered, and feminine; her wide mouth revealed white, regular teeth. Despite a strong Italian accent, her English was easy. I assessed her as eighteen or nineteen, and not incorrectly as a consular secretary. Her sexuality was totally uncomplicated.

We shared my wine. Her knowledge and love of Rome was unaffectedly enthusiastic as we walked arm-in-arm through the liberated streets. Her ready laughter was that of the fountains.

We reached my flat without plan or comment and the lamp she lit in the deep darkness before dawn seemed to bring the room to life, casting friendly shadows of the great bed on the old walls. Strangely this foreign room became home. We were alone in the world.

She turned down the bedclothes, carefully hung up my tunic, and put away my shoes before turning out the lamp. Briefly, as she drew the curtain, the beauty of her body was silhouetted against the dawn. Her love was fresh, passionate, almost maternal in its insatiable giving. Then she lay in the crook of my arm, her head on my shoulder, as we savored the joy of our love in the strengthening light.

When I awoke later, she was gone. No note, no name, nothing except the faint trace of her perfume on the pillow next to mine.

For two weeks I searched Rome. Every evening I combed the Via Veneto, scanning the crowd for the bronze gleam of auburn hair, the swing of a navy blue skirt, or the sound of her laughter. I retraced our steps from cafe to cafe, street to street, reviewing every word of our conversation in search of a clue as to her whereabouts. I knew then that the wonder of her love would always torment my nights, stealthily invade my waking thoughts, and tarnish any other love by the very power of its consummate totality. Finally I took refuge in wine.

The sudden gush of the bathroom tap flooded orange lights through my head. Kobie was fussing about the flat.

"Go away," I groaned.

There was a tinkle of crockery on the bedside table. From past experience I knew it was hopeless. Kobie snatched the covers off me in a quick merciful flourish.

"Good morning, Baas Paul!"

"Turn off that ghastly tap!"

Kobie gripped my wrist and guided my hand to the teacup.

"What time is it?" I croaked.

"Never mind, Baas Paul. You'll feel better after a bath."

"Let me warn you" — I wrapped the proffered towel

around my waist — "I can't stand any heartiness this morning." I made a silent oath never to drink wine again.

Kobie served my breakfast. "What is the Major going to do today?"

"I have no idea. Why?"

"Perhaps the Major would like to meet some people who have been very kind to me."

"Who are these people? Are they Italians?"

"You will enjoy it, Baas Paul. I have a car."

"Whose car?"

"They lent it to me."

"They lent it, huh?"

"It is all right, Baas Paul. The old man is very honored that I should bring my officer to visit their house. They are nice people, Baas Paul. They are not grand people, just good people. I think the old Baas takes a drop too much, but he's harmless, you know. Harmless."

A baby Fiat crouched cheekily at the marble steps of the villa. The years had left no trace of its original paint, and there was a rent in the worn canvas top. Kobie opened the door for me with a flourish, then folded his bulk into the tiny seat. With shoulders hunched and head bent, he steered proudly through the streets of Rome. I was amazed at his knowledge of the city.

Soon I lost sight of any familiar landmark and we were climbing steeply into the Palatine Hills. The road gave way to a mere track, and the Fiat slowed down to almost walking pace on the steep incline. Swerving suddenly, Kobie turned through a tumbledown gate. "We are here, Baas Paul."

The house on the rise was a flat-roofed adobe shack. A vine sprawled over a trellis. A cart with only one wheel leaned against a wall. Just visible around back of the house lay Rome, hazy blue in the distance. Kobie sounded the horn. Children rushed out of the door and ran shouting toward him. As he bent to greet the throng, a small girl threw her arms around his neck. At my approach they fell silent. Lifting a toddler in the crook of his arm, Kobie introduced the children.

"This is Major Pendrake," he said, and turning to me, "Baas Paul, these are Maria, Alberto, Anna, Giorgio, Italia, and this my special friend Piero."

The toddler buried his face in Kobie's shoulder. The other children acknowledged the introduction with wide uncertain eyes.

"These are all the grandchildren of old Lotticci."

"Where are the parents?"

"There is only one son alive, and a daughter; the others, four in all, were killed in the war. His son Giorgio is a prisoner of war in South Africa. He works on a farm."

"Really! Whose farm?"

"I do not know, Baas Paul. Papa Lotticci has forgotten the name."

"Hello, hello, hello!" A portly man with crisp curly black hair just graying at the temples lumbered from the house. The massive brass buckle of a leather belt perched precariously on the convexity of his paunch. His collarless blue shirt was open to the waist.

"Bon giornio."

"Bon giornio!"

The hand that gripped mine was the firm dry hand of a farmer. The old man beamed. He turned towards the house.

"Mama!" he bellowed.

Mama Lotticci was frail and looked old before her time. She bowed wordlessly as she took my hands.

And then Carla appeared from the house.

Experience cannot find words to define the conglomerate of rage, astonishment, passion, and betrayal, all combined to chill the blood, paralyze the limbs, and choke the breath with nausea as it wrenches at the fine balance of sanity. At that moment my only link with reality was the mute supplication in Carla's eyes. She stood there, the woman I loved, with my batman's arm affectionately around her waist. Her shock, I realized, was as profound as mine.

70

"This is the daughter, Baas Paul . . ." Kobie was saying. I could not speak. I nodded. A hot flush of relief suffused the pallor of her stricken face. She curtsied to me demurely.

Papa Lotticci broke into a torrent of Italian. The children hopped up and down, clapping their hands. The old man beamed expectantly into my face. I fought for control.

"He says we must come and drink some wine, Baas Paul," Kobie said.

Papa Lotticci waddled ahead while Carla and her mother turned and went into the house. The children skipped around Kobie. A trestle table had been set on the terrace under the pines. Papa Lotticci led me to a chair at the head of the table.

The vineyard, I recall, sloped steeply from the terrace. Far below, in the cleft of the hills, lay Rome and the silvery gleam of the Tiber. Papa Lotticci babbled incessantly and filled my cup with rich, red wine from the wicker-covered bottle. Carla and Mama Lotticci reappeared carrying platters of thick brown bread, macaroni and pizza, followed by salami and homemade cheese.

And later in the day, as the sun slanted in the west, the children sang as Kobie solemnly played the haunting Cape Malay melodies of our childhood on his mouth organ. His close-cropped black hair and straight nose looked typically Roman; the muscles of his strong neck were those of a statue anywhere in the city. Carla stood behind him with a hand on his shoulder.

Papa Lotticci nudged me. *"Loui avera multi bambina,"* he said with satisfaction.

It was dark when Kobie dropped me off at the flat. "Thank you," I said, "I enjoyed myself very much."

Kobie drew himself up to his full height and saluted. "Sir!" His face glowed with happiness.

"Take tomorrow off," I said from the doorway.

"Thank you, Baas Paul."

I watched the little Fiat roar up the street on its way to the girl in the Palatine Hills.

71

9

The end of the war, and Fiona — that was when the rot set in.

Is there anything quite so mentally fragmenting as the return of the soldier from a distant campaign? From years of totally uncomplicated commitment to disciplined camaraderie in the fight for survival, he is precipitated into desperate isolation. Somehow it is worse when he returns to a land which his crusade has protected from any exposure to the realities of war. As if coming round from an anesthetic, he finds long-cherished familiarities drawn in stark caricature. He finds himself an embarrassment to the society he has fought to preserve. He is deprived of both the sympathy and the bitter stimulus of rehabilitation which sustains the vanquished. Belatedly, he becomes aware that the fortitude with which people can stand the misfortunes of others is boundless, and he has more respect for his erstwhile foe than for his own kind. He knows then that mankind, like all nature, needs the periodic catharsis of flood, famine, fire, and war to survive. It is written that man must lose his life to live again.

Perhaps all would have been different if Kobie had been there, but his demobilization had been delayed in the bureaucratic chaos of peace.

It was a perfect spring morning, with Table Mountain etched pencil-sharp against an azure sky, as the Johannesburg train threaded through the points. Fresh sea air laden with memories of boyhood flooded the compartment. The civilian commuters hurrying along a suburban platform to meet their daily nine o'clock deadline were oblivious of the soldier returning from war. It was then, I remember, that the first vague sensation of extrusion from the world I had known niggled at my guts.

With a soldier's reflex I humped my kit onto the platform; and there beyond the barrier, slightly apart from the crowd, stood my mother leaning on Uncle Gert Cillier's arm. Her dark hair was streaked with gray and her smiling eyes sparkled with thankful tears.

Uncle Gert's heavy articulate hand fell on my shoulder. "Welcome home."

And Bella, my mother: "How are you? I cannot believe it is true. You have filled out. Where is Kobie? When does he get home? Grietjie is so excited she has taken to her bed — her rheumatism is terrible. Oh dear God, I'm such a lucky woman!"

Suddenly, with the instinct of experience and maturity, I knew what had been obvious for years — Uncle Gert loved and had always loved my mother. I thought of the girl Carla in Rome.

"It's good to be home," I said.

The flat in suburban Rondebosch was essentially the same. The polished table in the hall with a Chinese bowl full of freshly cut roses, the Regency striped armchairs in the living room, and the clean new blotter on the desk in my bedroom — all conspired to suffocate me. The sense of confinement made me feel graceless and unworthy of the welcome.

My mother took my hand. "You must come and see Grietjie."

The bundle perched on the old iron bedstead in the small back bedroom looked tiny and somehow shrunken. Grietjie's

73

face was buried in her twisted little hands. She rocked back and forth. "No, Miss Bella, no, Miss Bella, it cannot be true. I have seen it often. It may be a ghost."

The sniffing culminated in a long wail. I took the birdlike wrists and drew them gently away from her tear-stained face. Softly she touched my cheek. "My Basie, my Kleinbaas."

She brushed a slow rolling tear away with the back of her hand. A sniff twisted the little flat nose.

"Excuse me, my Kleinbaas, you must be hungry. Grietjie has new shortbread ready in the oven." With surprising agility she wriggled off the bed and hobbled to the kitchen.

"Be gentle with her, darling," my mother said. "It is quite a shock to be confronted with the answer to a constant prayer."

"It's wonderful to be home," I said again.

But it was not wonderful at all. The days when my mother was out teaching seemed interminable. Each evening I insisted on taking her out to dine, to a show, anywhere. Once I visited Fleur with Uncle Gert Cilliers. The house bore evidence of his loneliness. It was apparent that he used only the study and a small bedroom off the hall. The other rooms were shuttered and the furniture covered in dust sheets. The kelder was, as ever, immaculate.

"Now that the war is over we can expect Belle Fleur to come into its own again," Uncle Gert said.

The spirit of my father was all over the farm. I knew I was not ready.

"That will be good." I saw the look of disappointment in Uncle Gert's eyes. "I am not ready yet, Uncle Gert."

He put a massive arm around my shoulders. "Like wine, a man knows when he is ready. God willing, I shall care for Belle Fleur until you are."

Some days later I caught a suburban train to the city. To my delight I saw a familiar face on the crowded pavement — Allan Smith, looking very prosperous in a pinstriped suit. "Hello," I called. "I haven't seen you since we left school."

His eyes focused on my campaign ribbons. "Hello, it has been a long time, hasn't it?"

"When were you demobilized? How does it feel?"

Allan Smith tapped his briefcase. "Well, actually, my firm would not release me." He backed away. "Sorry to rush. Got an appointment and I'm late."

He stumbled into a passing woman. "Sorry, sorry." I watched him threading his urgent way through the crowd.

Spring flowers bloomed under the oaks in Government Avenue. I settled on a bench in the Public Gardens and lit a cigarette. A child shrieked in delight as a colored nanny rolled a ball across the sun-dappled lawn. Two squirrels chased each other round the bole of an oak. My mind refused to focus. Desperate loneliness engulfed me. If only Kobie were back. The afternoon loomed bleakly ahead. In the depths of dejection I caught a bus back to the flat in Rondebosch and threw myself on my bed. Just then the telephone shrilled in the hall with the welcome promise of human contact.

"May I speak to Major Pendrake?"

"Speaking."

"Oh! I wonder if you remember me? This is Fiona . . . Fiona Hackstone."

I racked my memory. "Oh yes, of course."

"Could you possibly come to a party tonight? Sorry it's such short notice but I've just discovered you're back in town."

I remembered her vaguely then. She had been a sprightly freshette at Varsity.

"Well yes, thank you. Where do we meet?"

"I shall pick you up at eight — three blasts on the horn. 'Bye now."

On the stroke of eight a horn blared in the street. As I came out Fiona moved over from behind the wheel of a vast black Cadillac. "Hello handsome!"

The flowing yellow hair I remembered was now piled on the top of her head in a firm braid. I slid into the driver's seat. The car was heavy with perfume.

"It was good of you to telephone. How did you know I was in town?"

"Oh, I've got my scouts out." Her voice sounded rougher than it had on the telephone.

"This is wonderfully luxurious — I'm more at home in a tank." I fumbled for the starter.

"Just press the accelerator," Fiona said. The enormous engine roared to life. "Isn't she a beauty? Daddy looks after her like a baby. He would have a fit if he knew we were using her, but he's in Johannesburg. Mummy is an absolute lamb. It was marvelous on convoy dances; we packed twelve into her at once." She giggled and moved across to put an arm through mine.

"You're bungy," she said, "just like the chaps on the convoys."

A little tremor of distaste registered in my stomach. I felt anything but "bungy." I made for the nearest parking space at the Mount Nelson Hotel and jerked on the hand brake.

"Careful — this isn't a tank, you know." She adjusted the rearview mirror, patting her hair into place. "You might have dropped me nearer the door; I'll be blown to bits."

"There's no wind tonight." I pointed to the motionless trees.

"Gallant, aren't you?" Fiona flounced out and slammed the door.

She was waiting for me in the foyer, and took my arm with a glittering smile. A flashbulb exploded in my face.

The rest of the party rose at our approach.

"Sorry I'm late," Fiona said, "but I've been crawling all over the slums of Rondebosch to round up this male."

They were all strangers to me — a man in a dinner jacket and his wife, and a boyish-looking naval officer with a girl whose face looked vaguely familiar.

"Have we all got a drink?" Fiona asked brightly.

"Bet your life, darling," the man in the dinner jacket said. He pointed to a slip on the table. "The card is waiting for your signature."

76

"I might have known." Fiona turned to me. "Nine-tenths of the liquor Johnny swills is at someone else's expense. Do sign it, like a darling."

The whole party found this desperately amusing. Johnny showed his teeth and brayed loudly. Conversation revolved round people who were unknown to me. I drank two whiskies in silence.

Fiona bounced to her feet. "Let's go and eat." She took my arm and led the way toward the restaurant. A horse-faced young man with lank blond hair sat at a desk.

"Good evening, sir — Miss Hackstone's party?" He selected a bill from a pile on the desk. "That will be twelve guineas, sir."

Fiona led the party to a table in the corner while I signed the check.

Dinner was excellent. Fiona and the girl on my left gabbled happily about parties they had attended, about some girl who had looked an absolute fright, about the Kahn party next week which was a must — Aletta Kahn's frock had cost four hundred guineas.

"Solly Kahn could worry," Johnny snorted, "He's filthy rich." Then of course there was Dawn's party at which Solly had taken off his trousers and danced a rumba.

"He has lovely legs," Fiona snickered.

I sipped my whiskey and thought of Carla in Rome.

"How long have you been in South Africa?" I asked the young sub.

"Just a week, sir," he said. He was enjoying a crepe suzette. "This is more than the people at home get in a month. Only a week and I've been absolutely feted — party every night. I can't believe it. It's pretty grim at home, you know."

"How do you mean, grim?" Johnny interrupted. "My wife has almost broken me sending parcels to Britain."

"They're a wonderful help," the sub said, "but we weren't all so lucky."

"Then get on my wife's list," Johnny brayed loudly. "One

77

more can't make any difference. I've got broad shoulders."

"Very kind of you," the naval officer said. "But things are looking up, thank you."

It was after midnight when the party broke up. "I'll drive," Fiona said. Her earlier concern for Daddy's car seemed to have evaporated. We tore through the sleeping city towards Sea Point with tire-screeching abandon. Fiona parked the Cadillac by the sea wall. A low moon gleamed on the glassy sea and a gentle swell broke on the rocks. I rolled down a window. The sea air smelt fresh.

"What are you trying to do?" Fiona asked. "Cool my ardor?"

In a moment she was in my arms. Her wide mouth sucked at my face. There were little grunting noises in her throat. All the frustration and disillusionment of those first weeks back home welled up in me. How I despised the silly little bitch! It would be good to squeeze, squeeze, and squeeze that silly neck until she died. I caught her firmly in my arms, throwing her across the wide seat.

"That's better," she moaned, "Look — look in my bag."

Grietjie woke me at nine with a cup of tea and the morning paper. "Miss Bella said to let you sleep late, Baas Paul."

Idly I glanced through the newspaper. My eye caught on the social page. There was Fiona's glittering smile, with me looking as I had felt.

"Miss Fiona Hackstone, that popular member of the younger set, and Major Paul Pendrake. Miss Hackstone was hostess at an intimate party of old friends. Also in the party were Mr. and Mrs. Johnny Dubet, and Lieutenant 'Pugs' McPherson, R.N., a popular visitor from overseas."

"Blast!" I flung the paper across the room.

Enough. I would call on the dean of the medical faculty as soon as possible.

10

"Man proposes and God disposes" — I shall never know when, where, or why this adage was imprinted on my memory but the slow rumble of the years has done nothing to reduce its credibility.

Dear God, dispose of me kindly today. I repent and I have paid my price.

Where in God's name was Stompie Lategan? Stompie and Stompie alone could get me out of this bloody mess. He had promised.

I glanced round the empty concourse. The riot squad men still stood immobile at the exits. One of the young men from BOSS leaned against a telephone booth. He was carefully biting a hangnail. The plane squatted passively on the runway. There was impatience in the aimless movement of the riot police on the tarmac. The crowd outside no longer sang. Only a low swelling murmur, an occasional shout, and the barking of a police dog confirmed the persistent menace.

"I am going to join the police force," Stompie had said that night. Thank God he had.

*   *   *

What a bunch we were in those days! In an effort to accommodate the influx of ex-servicemen who wanted to resume their interrupted studies, the University of Cape Town acquired a batch of redundant army huts and erected them in a vacant lot near the campus. The quarters provided cheap housing for men subsisting on army loans. Here, with two hundred others, I took refuge. The fact that we were together cushioned the shock of return to civilian and student life. We were older than the other students and richer in experience than those of the staff who had not gone to war. Some of us flunked out; others took to drink. There were wild nostalgic parties, drunks to bail out of police cells, and prostitutes to chuck out in the night. We had two laws — we stuck together, and we did not complain. The camp was affectionately known as Belsen.

Stompie Lategan's war had been harder than most. He was totally rejected by his rabidly anti-British family. The girl he had married before he went north to the Western Desert had run away with an R.A.F. aircraftsman and all his money. "I could forgive her had she picked a pilot with a D.F.C.," Stompie complained. "But an A.C. — God, Paul, those little bastards never wash their bloody feet!" The wound he received in the desert had left a livid scar from ear to nose across his left cheek.

Stompie was good for me. He had all the drive of the small man with none of the hang-ups. His approach to life was blithely practical. He possessed one old navy blue suit, and a patched tweed jacket he described as all-purpose. His shirts were what he termed communal. Each week he helped himself to a shirt from the wash line. At the end of the week he washed it, hung it out to dry, and selected another to avoid "favoritism."

Kobie, too, was home by then. He had bought a second-hand car with his war gratuity and gone into the taxi business. Each week he visited us at Belsen, polishing our shoes to dress-parade perfection, bringing fruit and fresh fish from the Salt River market.

Stompie came to my room that night. "I'm sick of bumming cigarettes," he said. "Now you can offer me one."

"How's the work?" I asked the universal question.

"It's coming on well." Stompie flopped on my bed. "Just three more years, Paul, then I'm free. Hendrick Christian Lategan, LL.B., will pay back his loan to General Smuts and join the police force, and never go to another bloody war."

"Oh, I don't know," I said. "I think I'd do it again."

"You'll never learn." Stompie blew luxurious smoke rings at the ceiling. "War! Pah! Who gives a bloody damn! The British are hungry as hell. The Germans are collecting rubble and eating garbage. The Russians are sitting in Berlin. The Japanese are smashed to hell, and you and I sit in this hen coop. What have we got to show for four years of our lives except this scar on my cheek? Nothing."

He continued his monologue while I coaxed my Primus stove for coffee.

"Join the army and see the world. Do your bit. Your country needs you. So you go to war. You see the world alright, from the back of a truck. You sleep in your clothes while you are being shot to hell. And then having done your job, my friend, you come home." Stompie watched his smoke rings twisting round the light. "They don't want to know about you or your troubles. The wise guys who stayed at home have got your job. A bloody little Pommy has been screwing your wife, and General Jan Smuts is messing about in England. Fine! Fine! He is an international figure but he owes them nothing. He owes me a hell of a lot. Sure he quelled a strike in Wales. I know all that. So I followed him into the war; but I, Stompie Lategan, need him now. What do I care about Germans, Italians, Russians, niggers, or even the bloody British? And, chum, what do they care about me?"

"Who do you think will win the next election?" I asked.

"The Nationalists," Stompie said. "I'm voting for them anyhow."

"What? You can't mean that!"

81

"I mean it alright. Look Paul, I'm a South African. This is my country. Who gives a damn about us? The British don't know how to live with niggers. This town is full of bastards the British begat by colored tarts they picked up in the streets."

"Really, it's not that bad."

"You'd be amazed. I went to a meeting last week. The Dominee Verwyt gave us the figures. Man, it was horrible. We've just got to stop the rot. Would you like your sister to marry a Kaffir?"

"No, of course not. I admit the British troops mucked in, but hell man, that was war. Believe me, a lot of European women we came across were no better."

"It was alright in the old days," Stompie said. "There was no foreign influence and they knew their place, but now I agree with the Dominee Piet Verwyt. They will swamp us unless we have apartheid. We have lived in peace with the blacks for three hundred years. We have not hunted, starved, swindled, and dissipated them into extinction as the Americans did their Indians. Our black majority has been here less time than the black minority in the States. Furthermore we did not drag them in as slaves. They were chased here by the Zulus from up north. Do you realize that we have nearly eighteen million blacks, a couple of million Cape Coloreds, and there are less than four million of us?"

"Not to mention the Indians in Durban," I said.

"Now there is a case in point," Stompie said. "Fifty years ago the English in Natal imported a few hundred coolies to work their sugar fields. Now there are nearly half a million, and they own half of Durban."

"We don't, and have never, mixed with them," I said. "For that matter they have never mixed with us. I don't like all this apartheid business."

"Something must be done. It should have been done long ago. The Dominee Verwyt says that General Smuts has just been putting it off for political reasons. We must act before it's too late."

"If we're so worried about the numerical discrepancy,

why don't the Nationalists encourage immigration?" I asked.

"That's all right as long as we get the right kind," Stompie said. "Dominee Verwyt mentioned that at his meeting too. It's no good them coming here and trying to teach us our business. They must come here prepared to be South Africans and do as we do. It's no good their arriving here and still talking about 'home.' Look at these Jewish refugees Jannie Smuts let in from Germany. Did they join the army and fight Hitler? Did they? Hell! They sat in Johannesburg and made money while Stompie Lategan was being bombed to hell in the Western Desert."

"But still, about this apartheid business," I persisted, "we've always tacitly accepted segregation. No decent colored wants to associate closely with a white or a black. The only danger has come from the occasional white and the worst of the coloreds. You can't legislate against that. At least they're on our side, so why should we antagonize them? Besides" — I hesitated to say it — "besides, some of our oldest white families are known to have colored blood."

"That's too bad," Stompie said. "But it's got to stop. Why, only yesterday, going up to Varsity on the bus, a colored girl got in and sat down next to me. All dressed up with a pile of books under her arm. I nearly climbed out of the window. That's where we Transvaalers can't understand you Cape people. In Jo'Burg the Kaffirs get off the pavement to let you pass. You people are too free and easy."

"Oh, come on. If she wants to take a university course, why shouldn't she? She hasn't done you any harm."

"You don't see the danger," Stompie said. "Believe me, they'll take all we can give them in the way of education and then they'll come to me and say, 'Mr. Lategan, I am a Doctor of Psychology and I want to marry your daughter.' "

I laughed. "Then you, Mr. Lategan, if you really object, simply say, 'Sorry, my man, but I do not give my permission and I am sure my daughter shares my views. Good morning.' "

"That's just where you're wrong, old friend," Stompie

said solemnly. "That is the moment when this black Doctor of Psychology, with his creeping Jesus Sunday suit, goes home and, next thing you know, you're a racist and he comes back, as naked as the day he was born with a dozen friends, brandishing assegais and making howling noises, and slits your throat from ear to bloody ear! And probably rapes your daughter for good measure! Dominee Verwyt assured the meeting that the Nationalists would make it a criminal offense to have intercourse with a colored person. He said that both parties would be put in jail. No nonsense at all, both of them."

"Where would you place Kobie September?" I asked.

Stompie was not amused. "You are being facetious about something which is really very serious. Kobie September is my friend. I owe him my life. Besides he grew up on your farm with whites. He has bought his taxi and he is doing his thing. He does not mix with blacks. Nor does he come here and pretend to be one of us. I respect him for what he is and I hope he respects me."

"My God, Stompie, these men who are pushing apartheid backed Hitler during our war. You know as well as I do that this apartheid rubbish is a political gimmick. They have simply backed the wrong horse and want to divert attention. Basically, as you well know, they are anti-British. If they get in, we will forfeit everything we fought to retain. What's more, the coloreds work in our midst. They do a great deal of essential work. It's not anybody's fault that they are here. What on earth is the sense of talking about apartheid when the whole structure of our lives is involved with them? Have you heard that there are black university graduates working on road construction for lack of better employment?"

Stompie stuck out his lip. "Have you heard that a brilliant white jurist is sitting here in this damn Belsen rapidly reaching middle age and broke to the wide? Have you heard that the plumber who came back from the war can't get a job because his apprentice is now the foreman, and the bank clerk finds that his prewar junior is now the accountant?"

"That is not the blacks' fault," I said.

"Then why should I worry if he's working on the road with his degree? What have you got to say to that, chum? The Dominee Verwyt took care of that too. You are white or you are not white." Stompie indicated the division with the edge of his hand. "We must have job reservation."

"Thank heaven there's no hope of the Nationalists getting in," I replied. "All this apartheid will do is to make an enemy of all non-white people, and unite them against us. It seems a high price to pay."

"You know, Paul, you surprise me. You come from one of the oldest families and yet you talk like an Englishman. Believe me, this is a dangerous business! We must build our nation and we must protect our heritage. You should have heard the Dominee Verwyt. 'One nation, one flag, one language, under the guidance of God.' Man, Paul, I felt a thrill down my spine."

"Balls!" I said.

"All right, all right." Stompie was indulgent. "You are allowing your personal prejudice against Dominee Verwyt to influence your thinking. For me, I'm voting Nationalist like all the other chaps Jannie Smuts let down. No bloody niggers are going to take my job away nor is any foreigner coming here to tell us how to run our country."

But Stompie was not alone. Dominee Piet Verwyt had been busy.

11

"Paul, I'm pregnant."

Even now, as I sit in this airport, the memory of Fiona's words that afternoon makes me go cold from my loins to the tips of my toes. My mouth goes dry, and my hands sweat. I can still, after all these years — twenty-six to be precise — smell the smoky stench of that public telephone booth at Belsen, see the grimy tattered directory hanging on a chain, the tiny spider busily enmeshing an unwary bug in a web by the naked bulb in the roof.

"Are you sure?"

"Of course I'm sure! I've had a frog test. Do you think I would be telephoning you if I were not sure?"

"Oh God."

"It has nothing to do with God. This is your fault. I have not told Daddy as yet but I am going to tell him this evening. He will be furious. He will want to see you." The line went dead.

Whatever the menace of modern technology or the demerits of a morally indulgent society, how different my life might have been — yes, and Fiona's too — had paternity tests been possible or abortion acceptable at that time. Perhaps it was just circumstantial, but never once from infancy to adulthood had Jeremy, my son, evinced one physical or psychological trait which might confirm my genetic contribution to his being. The doubt would always remain.

Utter horror blacked out my thoughts. I returned to my room to find a cigarette. Then I telephoned the taxi rank in the city. Kobie was there.

"Of course I will, Baas Paul. Things are slow this afternoon. Certainly Baas Paul, I would like to drive you out to the farm." He must have detected the stress in my voice. "Is everything all right, Baas Paul?"

"Yes, of course."

"I'll pick you up in twenty minutes. Goodbye, Baas Paul."

In the car Kobie looked at me anxiously. "Is Baas Gert ill, Baas Paul?"

"He is fine, Kobie."

"And Miss Bella?"

"It is important that I see Baas Gert at once," I said.

He spoke then of his satisfaction with his car. "No trouble at all and all paid up in two months." Of his enjoyment of the taxi business. "Fresh air you know, Baas Paul — something different every day, and people — all kinds of people, Baas Paul." Of his great fortune to have a room and board in the house of Achmat Salie.

Indeed this was not only fortunate but a great privilege, for Gammatjie, as all the world called Achmat Salie, was a legend. Achmat Salie had two religions — Islam and rugby football. Even in my boyhood Gammatjie had been an integral part of the Saturday scene at Newlands Rugby Ground. In red fez and spotless white coat, he had the unique honor of sitting at the players' entrance to the grandstand. When a player was injured the crowd would roar "Gamat! Gamat!" and the little figure would sprint across the field, white coattails flying, carrying his famous black box. It was said that there was healing magic in his gentle hands. Articles had been written about him in the weekend *Argus*, and he had a picture of himself standing between the

Springbok and the All Black captains. At Christmas he got cards from rugby men all over the world.

"He is a good man, you know, Baas Paul." Kobie glanced at me self-consciously. "And Fatima washes my shirts and mends my socks. Fatima is very particular, Baas Paul."

We sat in the study at Fleur, Uncle Gert and I. He was obviously stricken at my news. He lumbered to his feet and poured two glasses of brandy. "This, Paul my boy, is the worst bloody thing that can happen to a man." He gulped his brandy down and flung the glass into the fireplace. "God, I should know."

So that accounted for Aunt Hannah. "He met her on a hunting trip to the Transvaal," my mother had told me once.

Beyond the high sash windows the green rows of the vineyards stretched serene in the afternoon sun. Under the oaks by the kelder Kobie stood surrounded by eager colored children. He was handing out sweets from a paper bag. Shrieks of delight drifted on the breeze.

"Could this be your child?" Uncle Gert asked.

"Yes, it could be."

"Do you care for the girl?"

"No, Uncle Gert, I don't."

"Does the girl want to marry you?"

"I don't know, Uncle Gert. She simply said that her father would want to see me."

Uncle Gert pursed his lips and narrowed his eyes. "Well now . . . "He slapped his hands on the leather arms of his chair. "We must keep this thing in perspective. These things do happen. But God in His wisdom has arranged it so that it requires two adults to reproduce. You and this girl are equally responsible for its being. But do not forget that this child, if you are the father, has both Pendrake and Cilliers blood in its veins. There is no need for you to be on the defensive, and Miss Hackstone should be honored . . ."

"But Uncle Gert, what am I going to do?"

"You are going to do nothing. When Mr. Hackstone contacts you, you will not go to him. You will arrange to meet him here on this farm. This is your house and your farm. If he wishes to see you, Paul Pendrake, he may call on you here." Uncle Gert stubbed a finger on the arm of his chair. "And I shall be here. You see, I have met this man Hackstone. He came here from England just before the war. He started with a scrap metal and then a stevedoring business. Now he is buying up farmland wherever he can. He develops townships. I know, because he approached me to buy some of my land in Belville." Uncle Gert leaned forward in his chair. He drew down the corners of his mouth and shook his head. "They are not our sort of people, Paul."

"What shall I tell mother?"

"You will tell her nothing. I would rather you presented her with finality after you've made a decision. Remember, this may be her grandchild."

He walked with me to the car. "This is not going to be easy, Paul. Meanwhile, consider what your father Jonathan would have expected you to do. I have often found that consideration helpful when I am in doubt."

What a diplomat Uncle Gert proved to be!

All three of them came to Fleur that Sunday afternoon. They emerged from the long black Cadillac like hornets from a nest. Ernie Hackstone, short, bullnecked, and red-faced in a fawn checked suit, bounced up the steps. He was followed by Ma Hackstone, who wore that legendary English reserve which conceals nothing more than total self-absorption, and Fiona, petulant in a picture hat and pink cotton gloves.

Monumental in his church suit, Uncle Gert appeared suddenly at the top of the steps. *"Goie middag, Meneer,"* he boomed in Afrikaans.

Ernie Hackstone's nose stopped an inch from the middle button of Uncle Gert's waistcoat. Fiona and Ma Hackstone collided with Ernie's back, and Ernie stumbled to his knees.

"*Welkom, welkom,*" Uncle Gert beamed. "*Welkom op ons plaas.*"

Ma Hackstone's thin lips drew into a button like a cat's backside. "We don't speak Dutch," she hissed as she bent to lift Ernie to his feet.

"A thousand pardons!" Uncle Gert's face was the epitome of remorse and concern. "You are not hurt, are you, Mr. Hackstone?"

Irritably Ernie Hackstone shook his wife's hand off his arm. "No, of course not." He dusted his knees. I smiled at Fiona. At that moment, I recall, I felt sorry for her.

"Welcome to our humble home." Uncle Gert showed the Hackstones into the gracious hall and led them to the study.

Ernie Hackstone sat with his briefcase on his lap. Uncle Gert went to the liquor cabinet. "What may I offer you — tea, coffee, or brandy?" He dusted a bottle and held it up to the light. "It's only just . . ." — he squinted at the label — "fifty years old."

"Brandy," said Ernie and Fiona in one voice.

"I shall have tea, thank you." Ma Hackstone tweaked her silk frock over bony knees.

Uncle Gert pressed the bell. Right on cue a little colored maid staggered in with an immense silver tray, bearing my mother's best silver tea service, delicate avocado and cheese sandwiches, and *koeksusters.*

"You will, I trust, madame, forgive the rest of us if we don't join you." Uncle Gert smiled. "May I pour for you? Milk and sugar?"

Ernie Hackstone was peering through the window. I swear there was a grid across his pupils as he mentally cut the farm up into plots.

"Who owns this farm?" he asked Uncle Gert.

Uncle Gert took a swig at his brandy. "Why, my nephew Paul, of course." He lifted his glass to me.

"Now about this little problem we have." Ernie cleared his throat.

90

"Have we a little problem?" Uncle Gert folded his hands like a bishop. Ernie Hackstone opened and closed his mouth like a fish.

Ma Hackstone sat forward. "Tell him, Ernest, or I will."

"Well, we have only one child, you see, sir," Ernie said. "Fiona here — well, she is all Muriel and I've got. We're pretty cut up about all this. It's not that we want to make trouble or anything like that . . ."

I liked Ernie Hackstone at that moment, and I've liked him ever since.

"But it's just that I've got the brass, you see. I've worked pretty hard for it and, well, you see, it's just like this — we would like the kid to have a name." He cast appealing eyes at Uncle Gert. "You know what I mean, sir."

Ma Hackstone's mouth was small again. "It's not as if there isn't a legal side to the matter," she said. "We have consulted our lawyer."

I saw a flush and a swell of anger above Uncle Gert's collar. Damn it, I thought, this is my life you are all discussing. I had sorted it all out. I moved over to Fiona.

"Mr. Hackstone," I said, "I appreciate your calling on us today and I'm pleased to make your acquaintance. This child is as much mine as it is Fiona's. With your permission may I marry Fiona?"

"Oh Paul!" Fiona came across and took my arm. "May I, Daddy?"

There were tears in Ernie Hackstone's eyes. He held his glass out to Uncle Gert. "Let's have the other half."

Ma Hackstone sniffed.

Uncle Gert lifted his glass. *"Mag die weerlig jou slaan!"** He beamed at Ma Hackstone.

Within twenty-four hours my whole life changed. "The Hackstone Wedding" was cited as the wedding of the year. A sumptuous house was bought and furnished for the happy

---

* "May the lightning strike you!"

91

couple in Ma Hackstone's name. Two insurance policies were taken out on my life. They were ceded to Fiona, while I undertook to maintain the premiums. No monies were to be raised against the security without Fiona's specific written permission. "It's no more than Fiona deserves," said her mother.

There was the formal signing of an antenuptial contract which ensured that all wedding presents would be the property of the bride. "It is not as if your family are inviting any guests," Ma Hackstone explained.

And indeed my mother declined to do so. She received the Hackstones as she received my announcement of the marriage — with noncommittal grace. Uncle Gert had prepared the ground.

Only once, and then under extreme provocation, did she comment. "Your father described people like these as a travesty of their betters at home," she said.

My two lives had begun.

12

It was of course quite ridiculous. I feared it then and the years since have proved it: it is simply impossible for two beings of totally different cultural, emotional, and material background to cement a workable marriage. We were not even granted the temporary analgesia of the initial sexual romp which makes the early phases of some such unions tolerable. But I did try, and so I believe did Fiona, in those months preceding Jeremy's birth.

A study, complete with vast mahogany desk, and lined with books Ma Hackstone had bought as a job lot at an estate sale was provided for me. The gift of a secondhand Morris Minor to enable me "to get back to dear Fiona whenever possible" was bestowed "just until you start earning."

At least once a week, guests who were mostly strangers to me were invited to intimate little "dins." "Even if you have to study day and night we can't abandon our social life completely," Fiona said.

I felt humiliated, possessed, and trapped in a no-man's-land between two mutually abrasive camps. I hesitated to expose my previous friends, who would have been as ill at ease in my new environment as I, to my dilemma or to my sense of shame.

So I took refuge on neutral ground. Every so often, some-times early in the morning, sometimes in the late afternoon, sometimes deep in the night after a stint in the Casualty Department at the hospital, I would on impulse drive the Morris Minor to the taxi rank in the city, and if that proved fruitless, to the house of Achmat Salie in Chiappini Street, for a chat with Kobie. It was a custom which lasted twenty years and more. In the process I gained a new friend.

There was a timeless serenity in the house of Achmat Salie. I learned there that his father had been coachman to the previous governor-general. When the governor left for England, the house on Chiappini Street had been purchased and given to Gammatjie's father as a token of appreciation for long and loyal service. Following in his father's footsteps, Gammatjie had graduated from hansom cabs to taxis. He also helped Kobie get a contract with the Union Castle Steamship Company to drive English visitors on tours of the lovely Cape Peninsula.

One Sunday afternoon I walked with Gammatjie to the white-walled Karamat on the slope of Signal Hill. The wind, fresh in my face, whipped white horses across the sparkle of Table Bay. Below us, like a lace border on the cloth of Table Mountain, the city of Cape Town spread calm and serene.

"Tuan Said is buried here, Baas Paul," Gammatjie ex-plained. "He came to the Cape to keep the faith of Islam alive when Sheik Yusef died over two hundred years ago. I light three candles, Baas Paul — one green, the first color on Earth; one yellow, the color of the Prophet himself; and one white, the color of purity and spirituality."

And standing by that tomb, I imagined a great seventeenth-century ship rocking at anchor in the road-stead, the pennant of the Dutch East India Company flut-tering from her masts. Political exiles from Batavia, Sheik Yusef and his little band were sustained in this new land by nothing but their faith. They were destined to become the

94

skilled craftsmen — masons, carpenters, bootmakers, and tailors — of this remote victualling station on the long trade route to the east.

Never once in all those years, by query, implication, or reference, did Kobie or Gammatjie allude to my marriage. In this regard they extended the consideration one would to a friend who has lost a leg — ignore it and carry on as usual. For this I was grateful.

"Kobie has great news, Baas Paul," Fatima said one Sunday afternoon.

We sat in the cobbled back courtyard of Gammatjie's house in Chiappini Street. The high gables of adjoining houses diverted the buffeting southeasterly wind. The hot January sun filtered through the ancient trellised vine, casting mottled shadows on the whitewashed walls. In her magenta sari with fine white lace round its veil, Fatima sat beside me on the bench. Gammatjie squatted by the wall, a small crocheted skullcap on the crown of his head, his bare feet in wooden kaparangs. Kobie sat with his back against the door of his room, his legs stretched out on the cool stone.

For peaceful moments, only the rustle of Gammatjie's newspaper and the rhythmic click of Fatima's crochet needle against the ring on her forefinger intruded on the repose of the day.

The look on Kobie's face reminded me of those days at Fleur when Grietjie volubly rebuked him for circumstances he could not possibly help.

"Well, Baas Paul, I have a letter." He reached into the breast pocket of his shirt. "You remember Carla, the daughter of Papa Lotticci in Rome? Well, Baas Paul . . ." He was studying the letter. "You see, Baas Paul, it is like this . . . You know how it is. We have a child, Carla and I."

"What!"

"Yes, Baas Paul — we called our son Roberto. He is three years old, Baas Paul, and now Carla has agreed to be my wife. I have sent the money for the ship. They should arrive

95

in one month — on the Santa Maria. They sail from Genoa."

I thought of a warm generous mouth, soft breasts, gentle hands, the laughter of the fountains in Rome, and a totally giving passion. And a chilling sense of foreboding enveloped me.

"My God! How wonderful, Kobie. Of course I remember Carla well. Congratulations!"

"It is good, Baas Paul. Life is hard for people in Italy."

He passed me a snapshot of a child with the grave beauty of Mediterranean children.

"He is a lovely child, Kobie." I passed the picture back.

Kobie studied the photograph. "Here my son will have good food, warmth, love, and an education, Baas Paul." He smiled gently to himself. "Perhaps he will even become a doctor like you, Baas Paul."

Gammatjie looked up from his paper. "You should buy that house on Signal Hill, Kobie. Here in this Malay quarter there are too many strange people. It takes time to settle into a new country . . . You are a man of means now. Carla must have time to enjoy you alone."

"Will Carla not be lonely up there?" Kobie asked, and I knew that he craved support in his venture.

"If I may, I shall come and see her often," Fatima said.

"Have you seen the priest yet?" Gammatjie looked over his reading glasses.

"Yes, and I have promised the good Father that Roberto and any other children that Carla and I may have will be brought up in the Catholic faith."

"If the ship docks too late, Carla and the child may sleep here in our children's room until the priest is ready." Fatima smiled.

Kobie rose to answer the telephone shrilling in the house. As he passed he patted Fatima's hand affectionately. "Thank you," he said.

"Are you happy for him, Baas Paul?" Gammatjie looked searchingly at me.

96

"Are you, Gammatjie?" I stalled.

"Well, Baas Paul . . ." He furrowed his brow. "I think that each man should try to respect himself, his people, and his religion; he should respect the man, the people, and the religion that is different; but above all he must have the wisdom to respect the difference." He ticked the items off on his small delicate fingers.

"We can only pray for their happiness." Fatima crocheted intently.

Gammatjie spread his hands. *"Inshalloh!'* he said.

Kobie and Carla were already married and settled into the house on Signal Hill when Fiona, my baby son Jeremy, his nanny, and I returned to Cape Town from a six-week vacation — "for dear Fiona to regain her strength" — in Ma Hackstone's seaside cottage.

It took me a few days to pluck up the courage to visit the house on Signal Hill. My visit was precipitated by a chance remark made by Fiona. "That wretched colored man September, or whatever his name is, has been phoning this house incessantly for days. The last time I was nursing Jeremy. I told him to stop being a nuisance."

"Paulie, Paulie, Paulie!" Carla ran down the slope to meet me as I walked up the path. Heels flying and bright skirt billowing, she flung herself into my arms. Her embrace had all the mature spontaneity of the Mediterranean, and the poignant agony of all exiles when confronted by an association with their place of origin.

She had matured. The slender waist and hips had broadened, the wide high cheekbones and generous mouth were accentuated and classically chiseled. She looked lovelier than ever. Her auburn hair glinted in the sun.

Then, as she clung to me, I heard Kobie laugh. He stood, huge and happy, with the child clinging to his hand. Responding to the deep rumble of mirth and the obvious joy of the moment, the child was laughing too.

"Come and meet the gentleman, Roberto," Carla said.

"This is my son, Roberto, Paulie. Say good afternoon, Roberto."

The child took my hand and bowed formally.

"You must forgive Carla, Baas Paul." Kobie was still amused. "She is far from home and does not know our customs."

"Forgive, forgive," Carla said. "What is there to forgive?" She linked an arm through mine and collected Kobie with the other. Arm in arm we walked up the path to the house.

"How well and brown you look, Paulie! Kobie tells me you are married and have a son. She must be a very beautiful lady, your wife. May I see her soon? Oh, this is so very wonderful. How do you like our house? Is it not too *magnifico*? Mama would be so happy to see me now. All this space and the wonderful sea and the beautiful mountain. The setting sun is too wonderful over the sea . . . in the mornings we hear the doves in the trees, and there is a squirrel. Have you got squirrels at your house, Paulie? Oh how I wish Mama could see me now. And the fruit, the peaches and the grapes, and the fresh fish from the sea, and the meat so cheap! Oh how I wish Mama and the children could see me now."

She turned to Kobie and kissed him on the mouth. "Oh, I am so happy!"

I knew I was safely over the first hurdle.

13

"There is one thing it is not possible to fight, Paulie — that is love."

Nothing, I fear, will ever fog the memory of that afternoon in the house on Signal Hill. Perhaps it was the sinister gloom of the black southeaster which sharpened every faculty to exquisite agony. Neither winter's rain-laced northwest gales, nor summer's boisterous, sunny winds have this singular effect. But on that day the ominous clouds, unseasonably chilling but with no real promise of rain, obscured the face of Table Mountain and swirled round the shoulder of Devil's Peak to cast a strange sense of foreboding over the city. In the streets the few pedestrians went about their business with a lonely, almost furtive air. Traffic moved with sullen reluctance. Even the gulls left the leaden sky empty, to huddle flurry-feathered on wharf and pavement against the menace in the wind.

Perhaps it was the black southeaster which finally tipped the scales. I do not know. I do know that suddenly the leaden weight of desire outweighed every other consideration, and as I left the hospital I turned my car toward the house on Signal Hill.

I recall too the dryness of my mouth and the hammering of my pulse as I waited for Carla to answer my knock. Far

99

out on Table Bay a tanker, swell breaking over her bow, wallowed toward the open sea. From the Battery on the mountain the crack of the noonday gun thudded across the city.

"Paulie!" Carla kissed me gently on the cheek. "I felt in my heart that someone would come today . . . I am desolate with lonesomeness . . . Kobie has taken some tourists to Stellenbosch and Roberto has his choir lesson . . . This wind makes my heart so sad." She took my arm. "Come in out of this terrible wind."

Her auburn hair was loose over the velvety smoothness of her tanned shoulders. Her frock was bright-colored, and full-skirted below a tight-waisted bodice. She wore thonged Roman sandals on her shapely brown feet. The fragrance of her hair brushed my cheek.

"Paulie," she smiled into my face, "you look tired and so serious. Come in and sit down . . . Have you had food? I shall give you some lasagna, yes?"

"Thank you," I said, "I would like that."

She took my arm and led me into the living room. "You do not look right. I do not like you to be sad. Tell me what is the trouble today."

It was then that I threw discretion to the winds. My need for her was more than I could stand. "Carla . . . Carla . . . Why did you leave me that morning in Rome? I searched for you for weeks. Why did you leave me like that?"

There was a long silence between us then. She furrowed her brow and looked at me as if searching my soul. "Because, Paulie, I feared you might love me . . . It is not good for a man like you to love a girl like me, or for me to love you too much."

"For God's sake, Carla, why?"

She pursed her lips and sighed. "Because, my darling Paulie, I have been every man's woman. It was not my choice . . . but I had been like that. In Italy we believe in such things . . . we know of such matters. You were so young, so gentle, and so loving. It was better to keep the

100

memory of what we had beautiful than for time and society to make it ugly and a trap for us both. You are a gentleman, Paulie, of established family. I was not for you, my darling."

"But, Carla . . . surely you could have let me be the judge of that. At least you could have given me time."

She smiled at me kindly as if I were a child. "And when you did find me, Paulie?"

"Then you were Kobie's woman . . . the woman of my batman."

She turned on me, Latin anger flashing in her eyes. "And I am the wife of Kobie — your batman — and I am honored to be his wife . . . more honored than I or any other woman deserves . . . And he loves me and Roberto too."

Then I did what I shall always regret. Frustration, shame, and misery conspired, as they so often do, to seek relief in spite.

". . . and Roberto?" I asked.

Carla dropped her eyes and bit her lip. She turned and walked into the kitchen. "My husband," I heard her say, "is very proud to have a son like Roberto."

Except for the ticking of the clock and the boom of the wind, the house was still. I wanted to go to her in the kitchen but somehow I could not move. I sat there in Kobie's house, desperately conscious of the gulf that separated our lives. And the gulf was the prescription of my own false values, my addiction to compromise at every level. I was caught in a web of my own making. I felt humiliated, resentful, and desperate.

I heard the rattle of cutlery, and smelled the warm lasagna from the kitchen. Carla was smiling when she returned to lay the table for our lunch.

"Paulie," she said quietly, "we must not hurt each other. There are affairs of which we must talk."

"What is there to talk about?" I was petulant.

She came and sat beside me. She took my hand. "Do you know how much Kobie loves you? His love for you is beyond

101

words. It is greater than the love of a brother or even a father. He told me once that you, Paulie, are the keeper of his spirit. This man of mine would die for you. He does not call you Baas Paul or Master, or whatever it may mean, as a servant might do. He does so because of himself and his spirit . . .

"He speaks of your Uncle Gert Cilliers, your dead father Jonathan Pendrake, and your mother as we speak of the saints. This faith is as necessary to him as food is to other men. His love is for your family and his duty is to you. He would kill or die for this faith. To destroy this faith would be the death of Kobie."

Carla was stroking my hand.

"I loved you in Rome, Paulie, and you were gentle and there was a need for love in your heart as there was in mine . . . You did not take me in cruelty as the English do, or cry for your mother or girl like an *Americano* . . . So I loved you and was grateful for your love. I still love you. I know, Paulie, you are unhappy with your wife — for that I am sad — she has been very rude to Kobie and for that I hate her, and Kobie despises her because of his love for you. I know what it is that you need, Paulie — you need my love. If it were otherwise it would please me to make you happy, to comfort you with my love here, this day, in this house . . . but, Paulie, have you ever seen the anger in Kobie?"

"Yes, I have."

"I saw it too once," Carla said. "There was a black *Americano* in Rome — a big man with teeth like the keys of a piano — and Paulie, I had known this black man. When we met, he said to me 'Hi' as *Americanos* do to all the world . . . then this black man put his hand on my arm, Paulie." Carla's eyes grew wide and she put her palms to her temples. "Kobie changed into a lion — a terrible lion. He picked the black man up as if he were straw and threw him among his comrades. There was death in Kobie's eyes . . . In a minute the street was empty. I have never seen men run so fast. And Paulie, remember . . . I love Kobie. I love him more than my life. He is strong — strong as a wild bull with a woman, but with me he is gentle as a lamb — but if I were to deceive him, it would be death for me . . . not for you, Paulie, because his duty to you is necessary for his life. You would be safe, but for me and Roberto it would be death, because of my failure to honor his love." Carla's voice was beseeching. "Paulie, for my sake, do not require my love . . . Be my friend, Paulie, but do not require my love."

14

Election Day, May 26, 1948, dawned fine and clear. Technically domiciled at Fleur in Franschhoek, my vote was registered in the Paarl constituency. Largely at Uncle Gert's insistence, I had agreed to drive a car in General Smuts' support.

Election fever ran high in the town that day. Hannah Cilliers, resplendent in what she insisted was her grandmother's pioneer dress and kappie, drove into town from Drakenhof on a wagon drawn by ten longhorn red Afrikaner oxen which we later learned had been imported from the Transvaal for the occasion. Symbolic of apartheid, a tattered colored urchin led the span. *Die Vier Kleur*, flag of the old Transvaal Republic, fluttered defiantly above the wagon seat. I watched them unharness the team in the market square. A large bonfire was kindled. Mounds of mutton, beef, and good *boerewoers* were carried from the wagon and roasted in the traditional manner. All day Hannah Cilliers fed the crowd. In the afternoon she led the young people in a chorus of Afrikaans folksongs.

It was late in the afternoon when a premilinary count indicated that a Nationalist majority was certain. A stirring shout rose from the multitude around Hannah's wagon. I saw Dominee Verwyt clamber onto the wagon and call for silence. He was as gaunt as ever but the ginger goatee beard had grayed. His eyes were wild. He congratulated Hannah in front of all the people.

"In our hour of victory, let us not forget our women," he shouted. "Our Afrikaner women have not only given birth to our nation. Throughout our history, our women have inspired our men to great deeds as our sister Hannah Cilliers has done today."

Hannah seized the flag and waved it aloft. The young people sang "Sarie Marais."

Uncle Gert appeared at my shoulder. "Paul, I must get out of here. Please drive me. First to Drakenhof. I must pay the men."

We drove into the sunset in dismal silence. In the living room Uncle Gert poured brandy.

"She used my wagon without my knowledge," he said grimly. "What a fool I feel! The Cilliers have always been Smuts people. Why must she make a public exhibition of herself?"

We heard a car draw up and Hannah came in. There was sly satisfaction in the look she directed at her husband. Without further ado, she flung her kappie aside and settled herself beside the radio. She looked maniacal. She dragged off one of the new rawhide boots she had bought to complete her pioneer outfit, and scratched appreciatively between dusty toes.

"Sina," she yelled through the house, "bring coffee! Missus is thirsty." Then she took off her other shoe.

The voice of the announcer confirmed our mounting fear. General Smuts had retained most of the urban seats, but the slowly mounting country results were solidly for the Nationalists.

"Gah." Hannah spoke to the radio. "Gah." She stretched her fat frame, spreading grimy toes. She struggled vainly with the hooks of her tight bodice. Impatience overcame her. She clutched at the cherished garment, ripping it down to the waist.

105

"For God's sake, Hannah." Uncle Gert sounded desperate.

The music on the radio ceased abruptly. "We interrupt our program for the Standerton results . . ." It was General Smuts' seat. "National Party majority . . ." General Smuts had been thrown out by his own constituents.

It was too much for Hannah. She capered round the room, a triumphant, blowsy, barefoot figure in a torn pioneer dress. Her laughter was hysterical and horrible with hate. She spat a long gob of saliva into the innocent face of the radio.

"For God's sake, Hannah!" Uncle Gert crossed the room and gripped the front of her bodice in a massive fist, holding her still. "For God's sake!" He shook her.

She stood searching his face. Her eyes, I thought, softened for a moment. Uncle Gert released her suddenly and she staggered back, flopping on a settee. She looked around the room almost coyly. Her gaze settled on her bare feet. Her corns were red and swollen. She drew them under the hem of her gown.

I saw her then as she must have been when they first met. A simple, buxom girl confined on an isolated, Calvinistic, bushveld farm, confronted with a stallion like Uncle Gert.

"Come, Paul, we must go," Uncle Gert said.

"Yes, go!" Aunt Hannah screamed. She was on her feet. She grabbed a porcelain bowl and hurled it at Uncle Gert's head. He ducked and it shattered against the far wall. She was sobbing now.

"Go, go to that precious ladylike Bella with her education, and the airs and graces she learned from that Englishman she married. Airs and graces that steal other women's men. Go!" A brass table lamp flew across the room. "Go, and take the Englishman's son with you. I have my own sons . . ."

I followed Uncle Gert out into the night.

In my mother's flat Uncle Gert ground a newly lit

cigarette into an ashtray and searched his pocket for another.

"Christ, Bella, this election result is unbelievable."

My mother was working at her desk. "I rather expected it," she said. "There is usually a change after a war. The British threw Churchill out. Our soldiers came back to disillusionment. It is they who have voted the Nationalists into power."

"How can you be so calm, Bella? Everything we fought a war for will go by the board."

"It's not that bad," my mother said. "After all, this is a democratic country. If the Nationalists don't come up to scratch, the people will vote them out next time. I have great faith in the people."

"Democracy! Do you think these people will ever relinquish their grip on the machinery of state? They'll stop at nothing to retain it. Bella, you should know these bastards as well as I do. That wretched little creature Dominee Piet Verwyt with his kinky leg climbing onto my wagon. It would have been far better if Jonathan had let him die in the veld. All this rubbish about apartheid. Has it ever been necessary to have laws to keep our family white?"

"Of course not."

"No, but it is attractive to ignorant poor whites to be assured of protection against colored competition. Surely you realize there is no principle involved. Our problem is not a color problem. Our problem is white — white!" Uncle Gert flung out his hands. "Pro and anti-British."

He got up and paced the room. "I see disaster ahead, Bella. All this talk of Afrikaner culture. What is Afrikaner culture? A cult of people who trekked into the wilderness in ox wagons a hundred years ago because they were unable or unwilling to cope with the problems of an organized society. Were it not for the discovery of gold in the Transvaal at the beginning of this century, they would still be in the wilderness and probably all be colored. What is their culture? What contribution have they made?

107

"Their culture is that of the ox wagon, the resentful running away, the driving of their cattle into other men's land at night and denying it in the morning. Now these men are creating a past to justify their present aspirations and to explain future calamity. They are evil men, Bella — creatures like Piet Verwyt. Years ago they invited me to join their wretched Broederbond. Even then it did not appeal to me. General Smuts was right when he described it as a cancer in our land.

"For their own benefit, these men will isolate and exploit simple people by eulogizing their inferiority and build up a tidal wave of hatred among all colored people. Then, Bella, when the die is cast and the position is irreversible, these bastards, the Piet Verwyts, will get out with the money they have extracted and leave the people they have destroyed to cope with the mess."

"But Gert, my dear, you and I are South Africans. Our families have been here from the very beginning of things. My grandfather trekked to the Free State. My father was born there and so was your mother. We see through all this nonsense. Surely you do not imagine that we are alone? We are South Africans. This is not the end of the world. Every country has its political changes."

"Yes, we are South Africans," Gert said solemnly. "But although we speak Afrikaans, we are not acceptable as Afrikaners in Piet Verwyt's book." He looked thoughtful. "Tell me, Bella, how would you describe an Afrikaner in the modern sense?"

"Well . . ." — she considered a moment — "one who is born in South Africa and, I suppose, whose home language is Afrikaans."

"If that is the case, then you and I should qualify. Why don't we? We never shall because we are not afraid. No, Bella, my dear, the new Afrikaner is a man who hates every other white race, every colored race, every other religious denomination whether it be Anglican, Catholic, Jewish, or Baptist. But, above all, they hate the English. Especially

108

their English compatriots. They believe, or are led to believe, that their insecurity is the fault of the English. If they only knew just how little the English in Britain know, understand, or care about them, except perhaps for the cold comfort of feeling that there are countries where things are worse than in their own!

"These Nationalists pretend to be tough, independent, proud individualists, like your father and mine, but they will grind our people down to the size of their own cowardly cult. And when a new generation has been conditioned, reversal will be impossible. Our country will be governed by the sons of railway gangers and sour Dutch Reformed Church ministers, and we'll be isolated from the world. Perhaps, before the crunch comes, the English, the Jews, and some of those responsible for this folly, will take what they can and get out. Three centuries of human endeavor will revert to chaos and barbarism. But, mark my words, Bella, those who must stay will be held to account."

Ernie Hackstone was not disturbed by the Nationalist takeover. "Not at all a bad thing," he said. "There is this to be said for the Nationalists — they will fight socialism tooth and nail."

"You don't understand," I argued.

Ernie winked at me. "In the final analysis, it's big business that calls the tune. It has always been that way, and it always will be — no need to get your knickers in a knot."

"Politics don't interest me," Ma Hackstone said, "but I'm all for keeping these coloreds in their place. Why, only this morning Betty, the cook, gave notice. After all I've done for her."

15

Stompie Lategan graduated that year. He had applied for the post, or so I assumed at the time, and been appointed assistant commandant of the Police College in Pretoria. He was jubilant.

"Imagine a policeman with combat experience and a law degree! The sky's the limit."

In those few hectic days preceding his departure for Pretoria, there was neither the time nor the money to replace the tattered belongings of his student lifestyle. His few clothes were stuffed into a battered suitcase supported by twine, and his books into a cardboard carton.

He bade Kobie a casual, rather cool farewell, and refused the offer of a taxi ride to the station. "Baas Paul will drive me. Good luck, Kobie."

"Good luck, Baas Stompie," Kobie said. "I shall always remember you."

We had difficulty stowing his baggage in the Morris Minor. The string round his suitcase snapped and had to be repaired. In the process Stompie dropped a large manila envelope, scattering papers all over the car. We made the train with just minutes to spare. I can see him now as he waved from the compartment window, clutching his manila envelope.

The next day, as I braked sharply at a traffic light, a folded sheet of paper slid out from under the seat of the Morris Minor — a simple white foolscap sheet. I assumed it was one of mine and picked it up. It was typewritten. There was no heading — just "No. 902" in the top corner. I read:

Not for a moment must we allow the recent election victory to lull us into complacency. The Nationalist Party has won by a narrow margin. The long preparation of the thirties when we nursed our members through the economic depression has paid dividends. But let us not forget that we have had the discontent of the returned soldier to exploit, and the general fear of the colored races to divert attention from the main issues. The tendency of the English to abandon their hard-won empires to savages and their own nationals to ruin has lent reality to this fear.

Apartheid has proved to be a magic word.

We have reached the stage when the magnitude and diversity of our task is far too great for this executive alone to handle effectively. At this time we have roughly 9000 members distributed over 600 cells throughout the country. As always, the three main bastions of our cause are vested in the Nationalist Party, the Dutch Reformed Church, and the Afrikaans language. The time has come for us to consider delegating our authority for the better promotion of our task.

1. *The Federation of Afrikaans Cultural Societies:* This body embraces the propagation and promotion of all purely Afrikaans interests under cover of culture. This nucleus will now control an Academy of Science to promote purely Afrikaans university education, as well as the personnel of the huge railway and postal departments. Using the necessity of bilingualism judiciously, it should be possible to ensure a majority of totally loyal Afrikaans personnel in all departments of the civil service. Further, this nucleus will establish banking houses, chambers of commerce, and financial institutions. They will also establish liaison with carefully selected members in the British colony of Rhodesia.

111

2. *Youth:* National youth movements require particular attention. Afrikaner youth must be given a special objective, a national incentive, and constant educational conditioning. A special movement which will provide a recruiting ground for our successors will be established. This body will be called Die Ruiterwag.

Steps will be taken to ensure that our Afrikaner youth is protected from contamination by association with English youth. To this end, legislation will be introduced ensuring that Afrikaner children attend Afrikaans medium schools, and English children attend English medium schools. As to immigrants, the children of certified English immigrants will attend English schools. The children of all other immigrants will attend Afrikaans schools.

We must ensure that the teaching profession at both school and university level is totally controlled by loyal and active members. The same principle must apply in the other professions. Our aim is total Afrikaner domination with Afrikaans as the official language.

3. *Delegation:* It must not be forgotten that delegation of control may constitute a weakness. To avoid this weakness, it is suggested that we constitute a watchdog system. A network of men will be designated to report to this executive directly. Task forces of such men can keep a close watch on cabinet and public service operations to prevent any backsliding, lack of enthusiasm, or deviation from policy.

We refer particularly to our policy with regard to Africans, coloreds, youth planning, religious defensibility, sport, communism, and the English-speaking section where the dangers of liberalism lurk in the ranks of Catholics, Free Masons, Rotarians, Boy Scouts, and allied subversive organizations.

To ensure loyalty, it is suggested that these watchdogs must be guaranteed continuity of service for life. New blood may not be reliable and retirement may be resented. These men must all hold influential positions in public life, so as to exercise their political influence to best advantage.

4. *Apartheid:* Apartheid has captured the popular imagina-

112

tion. Now it is essential that it be put into positive effect. It is appreciated that this executive will never gain the support of the Cape Colored people. To this end, all further propagation between whites and coloreds must be stopped. The Nationalist cabinet will introduce an Immorality Act, making carnal intercourse between whites and non-whites illegal. A further act, the Mixed Marriage Act, will prohibit marriage across the color bar. The penalties for contravening these acts will be imprisonment for both parties without the option of a fine.

A population register will be compiled. Each person will be required, by law, to carry an identity card labeling him white, colored, Indian, or black. Before any man may accept work, or eat in a public place, or attend public gatherings, he must produce his card proving his qualification to do so.

5. *The English-Speaking Section:* It is the contention of this executive that we will never Afrikanerize these people, nor the Catholics, nor the Jews, nor any immigrants except the most simple workers who are no better than our coloreds. These people, the Jews, the Catholics, and especially the English, are our enemies.

As I read, I felt a dreadful sense of betrayal. Stompie Lategan was Broeder No. 902 in the notorious Broederbond. I recalled Uncle Gert's words: "a cancer in our land." My first impulse was to tear the document to shreds. Instead I folded it, and when I got home, put it in an envelope, sealed it, marked it "Stompie," and locked it in a drawer of my desk.

Three days later, Stompie was on the telephone. "Paul, you remember I dropped my papers in your car when you drove me to the station. Did you find anything in your car?"

Let him stew, I thought. "No, I didn't."

"Oh," Stompie said, relief in his voice. "Well, never mind. I thought I would ask. How are things?"

"Just fine," I said. "Just fine."

113

16

"I am not leaving Cape Town." Fiona was very definite. "Can you imagine me in some godforsaken Afrikaner dorp, earnestly baking milk tart, bottling preserves, and frantically knitting with a bunch of overweight peasant women? Besides, there's Jeremy's education to consider. You must be mad to contemplate such a possibility!"

Opportunities for medical school graduates were few and far between in 1952. A disproportionate number of local graduates and a massive influx of refugees from nationalized medicine in England had temporarily saturated the market. Though I had to agree that Fiona's sentiments were valid, they did rather narrow the field.

"What about Reggie Bentwhistle?" she suggesed. "I gather he wants a partner."

I had seen the advertisement and made inquiries. As a South African, Dr. Bentwhistle had escaped call-up in England, and by good fortune had managed to get a passage to Cape Town during the war. He had no reason to regret his decision to return to the land of his birth at a time when doctors were in short supply, and being from a famous medical school in England still carried remarkable prestige in colonial-minded Cape Town society.

I made an appointment to see him two days later.

"You say you were actually born in this country?" Daphne Bentwhistle smiled her special smile. She held her head slightly to one side, and the afternoon sun filtering through the window of their drawing room shimmered through her peroxided hair.

"Yes indeed."

"How very remarkable. Actually Reggie was born here too." She lit a cigarette. "But then of course he was sent home to school, and of course to Guy's in London. He's a Guy's Hospital man, you know."

"This is a charming room," I said. "White is so cool."

"I'm glad you like it. Of course we had to import all the stuff, but one has to create one's own atmosphere, hasn't one?"

She excused herself to take a telephone call in the hall.

"The doctor is still out," I heard her say. "No, I don't . . . I don't expect him until late. He is so frightfully busy. Well . . . no, I couldn't possibly recommend anyone else. It really is awfully difficult. Perhaps you could try again later. He may be able to fit you in somehow. Goodbye."

"These diplomatic people are the end," Daphne said as she returned. "Quite fun but so frightfully foreign. They all dote on Reggie. It's utterly exhausting. But then they're so desperately far from home, aren't they? Thank God they have him to lean on."

I looked at my watch. "It's after seven; perhaps I should come back some other time."

"Reg is always late," Daphne sighed. "He'll be so disappointed not to see you. Can you stay to dinner?"

Dr. Reginald Bentwhistle proved to be a dapper little man with disproportionately short legs. He wore a pinstriped suit and a club tie. His dark hair was plastered down. Slightly protruding teeth and pale blue bulbous eyes made him look like a well-groomed guinea pig.

"Sorry old man." He shook my hand. "Today has been a succession of alarms and excursions. Simply too dreadful. It never stops." He wrinkled his nose and furrowed his brow, then turned to his wife. "Any calls, my dear?"

"Thousands," Daphne said, "but I've stalled them all. Now sit down and have a drink. You must consider yourself a little."

"What would you like?" Dr. Bentwhistle indicated a tray of drinks.

"A beer, thank you," I said.

"So you would like to join me in practice?" he inquired benignly as he poured his whiskey. "It's awfully hard work, you know."

"Well, yes," I said.

"Is that to your liking?" He passed my beer. "We've really had awfully bad luck." He turned to his wife. "Haven't we, my dear?"

"Quite shocking," she said.

"I'm sorry. In what way?" I inquired.

Reginald Bentwhistle shrugged his shoulders and straightened the creases of his striped trousers.

"Well, we had a chap here recently, quite a good fellow really, but you will appreciate that this is rather a — how shall we say — different practice. Not society — I hate the word — but, well, I have no patients in my practice whom I wouldn't enjoy having to dinner. All jolly good types who can afford a certain standard, and have a right to expect it. You do see my point, don't you?"

"Yes, I think I do."

Bentwhistle hitched himself forward in his chair. "Well, just to give you an example. This chap who was with me held the fort while I was away on holiday. That, of course, is the beauty of a partnership . . ."

"Provided the practice does not suffer," Daphne interrupted.

"Exactly! Do you know what this chap did?" Reggie pursed his lips. "He did a confinement on one of my patients. A very tricky business. He ruptured the membranes, and did an episiotomy. It was an occipitoposterior.

116

Imagine! Then there was a retained placenta. All on his own without consulting a specialist. I got back to find the woman and her husband doting on him."

"They have been Reggie's patients for years," Daphne said. "Absolute cream of the practice."

"Just imagine the stink if something had gone wrong!" Reggie looked aghast. "One just can't afford that kind of thing in this practice."

"Then there was that business with the Bland-Cootes," Daphne reminded her husband.

Reggie looked pained. "This man, a city councilor, was told — told, mind you, in so many words — to stop drinking."

"*Was* he drinking?"

"Like a fish, old boy. But you can't go around telling people things like that. Now, of course, I've lost him. They've been on my books for years with six children who were always ailing one way or another, but far worse, they have a wide circle of friends. Things like this get around, you know."

"Of course, you married Fiona Hackstone," Daphne smiled again.

"Yes," I said.

"Wonderful, old boy!" Reggie Bentwhistle beamed. "That will give an immediate entree. We shall move more or less in the same circles, shan't we?"

"Of course in this practice we have to work for a living," Daphne said pointedly. She was beginning to grate. Reginald gave his wife a sharp look.

"You do speak Afrikaans, don't you?" he asked me.

"Well yes, rather better than English."

"Capital, old boy, although looking at you I'd never have suspected. Can't speak a word myself. It really is an awful bind because just recently quite a few Afrikaner families seem to be moving into this area. Sign of the times, I suppose . . . Mainly below the railway line, of course. You wouldn't mind coping with them, would you?"

117

"Not at all," I said.

"Fine, old boy, absolutely fine! Then of course, providing all else fits, there is the matter of a premium." Reginald Bentwhistle inspected his polished nails. "The usual sort of thing — you know, one year's income and all that — is hardly applicable here. This is just not that sort of practice. I'm sure you will agree. Five thousand pounds for a third share," he said. "Jolly reasonable, don't you think?"

That was how I made another compromise.

17

Where does human responsibility begin or end?

Is the casual passerby who passively watches a child screaming in the window of a burning building any less accountable than the psychopath who kindled the blaze? I wish I knew the answer.

My practice flourished. I got my honorary hospital appointment and really rather enjoyed the privilege of attending the Afrikaners who had moved into the area, albeit on the wrong side of the tracks. And I welcomed the ever-increasing demands of work which provided both Fiona and me with valid reason for pursuing our very different tastes.

Among mine were frequent visits to the house on Signal Hill. I do not know what, if anything, Kobie had told Carla, but after that first day she made no further mention of my marriage. I became a sort of honorary brother — I think that best describes it — and I can only pray that my visits returned some measure of the solace I derived from the privilege.

Perhaps it was unrealistic to expect their happiness to be immune to circumstance, but desolate as I was, my spirit was sustained by the timeless wonder of a simple love which only grew with adversity, and which condoned my passive observation of their plight without reproach.

Carla reveling in the undreamed-of luxury of a home of her own, delighting in the miracle of a radio, a refrigerator, an electric stove, and a car; Carla adapting Fatima's intriguing Malay recipes to her own taste; Carla tending her garden, enjoying the freedom and luxury of space; Carla slightly awed by my mother, whom she persisted in calling "Milady," and mischievously spontaneous in her affection for me; Carla profoundly grateful for the blessing of a husband and a child, giving thanks to God in the Catholic church.

How I envied Kobie!

In the beginning at least, Kobie shielded Carla from the impact of political change. How could he explain the unforeseeable nightmare which threatened to engulf them? How could anybody explain to anybody? He was haunted by fear that Carla might suspect him of deceiving her. How could he admit to her that when the Classified Population Register became compulsory, he had taken her passport photograph and registered her as colored? The clerk behind the grille had said, "What a pretty meid!" How could he tell her of the indignity of leaving the taxi rank where he and Gammatjie had worked for years for a segregated non-white rank?

And Roberto, their son. Roberto attended the kindergarten two blocks from their house. Carla saw the child to school and fetched him home for lunch. Roberto loved the school, and the teacher told Carla that he was "very clever, and with such good manners."

One Sunday afternoon Kobie and I stood on the verandah, watching Carla chase Roberto between tall stone pines. As she caught the child they rolled together on the grass, shrieking their delight. Roberto's black curls were tossed in the wind.

Kobie passed me the newspaper, indicating the headline. "FINAL PROMULGATION GROUP AREAS ACT," I read. "Residential areas zoned on basis of Color Classification."

"This house is in a white area, Baas Paul. What shall I do?"

"Surely they will be reasonable," I said lamely.

The businesslike arrival of a policeman at the house across the road interrupted our talk. He was talking to a white man who pointed in our direction. The policeman touched his cap, crossed the street, and came up the path. Carla and Roberto sat wide-eyed under the pines, watching.

The policeman was obviously one of the newly recruited Afrikaner youths. He had a small head, big ears, big feet and hands. His uniform hung on him like a sack. The leather belt and holster were dull, the brass buckle unpolished. A remarkably prominent Adam's apple gave him a heron-like appearance.

"Middag, Meneer," he addressed Kobie. "Have you got a a boy working here by the name of . . ." — he consulted his notebook — "September?"

Kobie introduced me. "This is Dr. Pendrake."

The youth wiped a limp hand through mine, and then held out his hand to Kobie. "Constable Barnard," he said.

"Mr. September . . ." Kobie said, glancing toward his wife and child on the lawn. "Constable, won't you come inside? Perhaps I can help you."

The policeman removed his cap and placed it on the floor. He drew out one of Carla's dining chairs and sat down.

"Have a cigarette." Kobie offered a pack.

"Dankie," Constable Barnard said. "You must excuse me but I don't speak English too good."

"Never mind, we can speak Afrikaans. How can we help you?" Kobie asked.

"Do you know, Meneer," Constable Bernard shut his notebook with a snap, "I wonder sometimes whether that sergeant at the station is not mad." He tapped the notebook. "Here he gives me a name September, and an address which has nothing to do with the crime."

121

"What crime?" I asked.

"A report has been received that a colored person with a colored identity card has sent his child to a school which, according to regulations, has been registered as a school for whites only." Constable Barnard grinned ruefully. "And the sergeant gives me your name. Is it not stupid?"

"Yes, it is," I said.

Constable Barnard crossed his legs and flicked the ash from his cigarette onto the carpet. He addressed Kobie. "But then it would surprise you what these coloreds will try and get away with, Meneer. Just last week, Meneer, I arrested a man with a colored woman. She was as white as you are, but the sergeant had been watching her for a long time." He sighed. "Ag, I felt so sorry for the man, Meneer. He cried like a baby. He was a deacon of the Dutch Reformed Church with six children." Barnard slapped his knee and winked. "God, Meneer, that woman was a beauty. They say these meids bite and scream like mad things when they are on the job."

Constable Barnard's long yellow teeth seemed to leap out of his face. He broke into a loud falsetto laugh.

Kobie rose to his feet. I could see he was fighting for control. "I am sorry we cannot help you," he said.

But Constable Barnard was in no hurry to go. He stubbed his cigarette out on one of Carla's plates. "You know, Meneer," he said, "this place makes me homesick for Knysna . . . that is the place where I was born. Perhaps if my back gets worse, the department will transfer me back home. It's worth a try anyhow, not so Meneer?" He shook my hand. "Well, goodbye, Meneer."

We watched him walk whistling down the path. Carla and Roberto were coming towards the house. Kobie gripped the post of the verandah. His cheek was against the cold iron.

"Christ almighty," I said.

"Don't talk, Baas Paul. Don't talk."

I saw that he was weeping.

18

"What am I going to do, Baas Paul?"

"Surely they will be reasonable, Kobie."

He had asked me for no more than advice, and I responded by mouthing platitudes. I knew damn well they would not be reasonable. I felt concerned, inadequate, and somehow perfidious. Awake or asleep, consulting or operating, I was haunted by Kobie's face as he clung to that post.

I arrived at the non-white taxi rank in the city just before seven in the morning. Both Kobie and Gammatjie were there. Kobie was giving his big black Dodge a final polish. Gammatjie sat quietly on a bench.

"Morning, Baas Paul," Kobie called.

"Good morning, Kobie."

I parked the car and moved across to Gammatjie.

"Not there, Baas Paul," Kobie said as I was about to sit down. "Let me fetch this bench." He dragged a heavy wooden bench marked "Whites Only" ten feet and placed it next to Gammatjie's.

Greenmarket Square was cool in the slanting shade of the tall buildings. The granite cobblestones, still moist from the drizzle of the night, smelled friendly. A vendor of second-hand books was setting out his wares. The bright awning of his stall caught the light. The elegant Old Town House, pride of the Historical Houses Commission, smiled like an aged dowager among the gauche, gray, corporate buildings which had invaded her world. The happy cries of newspaper vendors, darting among the early morning commuters, vied with the shrieks of seabirds wheeling against the sky.

Gammatjie drew my attention to a column in the newspaper he was reading, under the headline "Population Registration Amendment Bill."

Under this act a Japanese must be treated as a White under the Separate Amenities Act, as Other Asiatic under the Population Registration Act, and as Colored under the Mixed Marriages Act. At the same time, the Japanese are not Colored under the Colored Cadets Act and are not White under the Immorality Act. Under the Group Areas Act, they are not Asiatic or Other Asiatic, but must be treated as White.

"At least *we* know where we stand, Baas Paul." he said. I simply shook my head in disbelief.

Gammatjie tipped his tasseled fez back on his forehead and deliberately recrossed his legs. "We have been thinking, Baas Paul," he said. "Kobie must tell Carla. There is no other way."

Kobie folded his duster and sat down next to Gammatjie. "What am I to tell her?" he asked.

Gammatjie sighed. "You may start by telling her that I too have received a letter. A letter, yes, and many visitors too. A letter informing me that because of the objection of certain Afrikaner players and certain rugby clubs and in conformity with the new apartheid laws, I am no longer allowed to do my first aid at the Newlands Rugby Ground. Six Springboks of the old days have been to my house to say that they regret that there is nothing they can do. The law is the law. Two rugby clubs have brought me an address expressing thanks and goodbye, but these I do not want. A man does not need written evidence of his sadness. Not to be

124

impolite, for they mean well, I have accepted them and burned them in Fatima's stove. Tell her that." Gammatjie sighed. "It is always a comfort to know that one is not alone in times of trouble."

"Christ!" I stared at the white throng filing by unmindful of the tragedy being enacted on this bench. There were no smiles on the passing white faces. The only laughter in the square this morning was that of two old colored cleaners, cackling as they shook out their mops on the steps of Shell House.

"Tell her," Gammatjie continued, "that the Malay quarter where the house of my father is built will also become a white area and I shall have to leave. Tell her that many of our mosques are in danger. For a Moslem, it is not possible to abandon a mosque. Even if the building is destroyed, the ground remains sanctified as a mosque until eternity and Moslems are entitled to pray there at all times. Tell Carla that the white men who have come to power in our land do not know that the differences between men are those of quality and not of color. Am I, Achmat Salie, the same as that man?"

Gammatjie pointed to a drunken white bum weaving his way along the pavement. The man was middle-aged, bloated, unshaven, and ragged.

"But that does not mean we must deny brotherhood," he continued. "The faith of these men in power is that of fear. Having no dignity or goodwill themselves, they do not concede it to others. But do not fear, this time will pass. All we must do is try to avoid confrontation until time and the will of Allah teaches them dignity."

"How does this help my child?" Kobie asked. "It will be difficult enough to explain to Carla. What do I tell my child? Already this morning he is in tears because I have told him that he may not go to school."

"Who was your father?" Gammatjie asked suddenly.

"Why do you ask?"

"The law is very strange, but I believe it is possible to apply for reclassification to white. I am a Moslem, but my

125

blood is pure Malay and so is Fatima's and our children's
too. But you, Kobie, are as white as any Afrikaner. Your
body is big and strong, and your hair is straight. Your wife is
Italian and your child is a white child." He reflected a
moment. "But you still need advice. You remember old
Mrs. Ratz who has the little shop at the corner of our
street?"

Kobie nodded.

"Mrs. Ratz has a son, Hymie. He is a nice boy. He used to
play with my children and deliver the bread and come for
rides in my car. He is a lawyer now and I believe he helps
people in these cases. He is very clever. He is just starting
practice. Perhaps you could talk to him."

The telephone bell on the lamp-post rang. Gammatjie
walked across to take the call.

"Will you come with me, Baas Paul?" There was hope in
Kobie's eyes.

"Well, I don't know . . ." I began.

"Go with him, Baas Paul," Gammatjie said as he sat
down.

Hymie Ratz assessed us through his thick lenses. He rose
behind the littered desk and offered a puffy hand. We introduced ourselves.

"Please sit down, Mr. September." He drew up another
chair for me.

"Well, Mr. September?" Hymie beamed. "What can I do
for you today?"

The rickety old bentwood chair creaked as Kobie sat
down. "I have a problem, Mr. Ratz."

"Everyone has problems. We are here to sort them out.
And you, Dr. Pendrake?" Hymie Ratz wanted me clarified.

"I'm just a friend," I said.

"My problem is one of race classification," Kobie began.

"That is a very common problem these days. Who are
these people you wish to assist?"

"It is I who needs your advice, Mr. Ratz," Kobie said. "I

126

am registered as a colored. We have a child and a house. How do I stand?"

Hymie sat back in his chair. "What age is your child?"

"Roberto is six."

"Good. Then we need not worry about the Immorality Act or the Mixed Marriage Act." He pursed his lips and placed the tips of his pudgy fingers together. "These cases can be very involved. They take a great deal of careful preparation. It can prove to be a very expensive business."

"How do we set about it, Mr. Ratz?" Kobie asked.

"It depends on how much you can afford. What are your assets?"

Kobie thought for a moment. "I own my house up on Signal Hill, three taxis, and I have just over seven hundred pounds in the Standard Bank."

Hymie was noting it all down. "Any bond on the house?"

"No, and I've paid off the mortgage."

"Well, you're obviously a man of means." Hymie smiled. "If the case is carefully prepared, we can probably manipulate the intricacies of the law. I recall a case which was absolutely sewn up, but the Board refused the application simply because it was badly presented. Many of my colleagues don't know the ropes."

"Well, what do we do?" Kobie was impatient.

"Not so fast; not so fast!" Hymie held up a restraining hand. "In your case, I'm sure there'll be no difficulty. But, one never knows. You must understand that I cannot guarantee success. For this reason, it is customary to have a deposit before any work is undertaken."

"How much do you want?" Kobie asked.

Hymie pushed his luck. "I would suggest a deposit of, shall we say, two hundred guineas. It's quite usual, you know."

Kobie drew out his checkbook and proffered the amount.

Hymie Ratz scrutinized the check before slipping it into his pocket. He drew a pad toward him. "Now we can get down to business."

127

The lawyer made a note of Kobie's age, address, and occupation.

"Now, your father?" he enquired.

"I do not know who my father was," Kobie said.

Hymie Ratz sat back. "It is essential to know this. Is your mother still alive?"

Kobie nodded.

"Well, surely she should know."

"I shall ask her," Kobie said. "Of course, it will not be easy, you understand . . . so before I do that, will you please outline the procedure, Mr. Ratz."

"Well, after all the facts are collected, we make out a case for presentation to the Race Classification Appeal Board. If that is successful, we have succeeded. If not, we appeal to the courts. The bench is often most sympathetic. No political slant, if you know what I mean."

"I see."

Hymie Ratz rose to his feet. "Well, as soon as you tell me who your father was, we can proceed. When do you think you'll have the information?"

"I shall have it on Sunday."

"All right, then. Monday at the same time?"

"We will not worry Miss Bella with this, Baas Paul," Kobie said as he left me on the pavement. "Miss Bella will not like it at all."

On Sunday morning Kobie, Roberto, Carla and I waited for Grietjie at the bus stop. The bus appeared right on time, and drew up at the curb.

"Come on, hurry up there!" the conductor yelled up the stairs leading to the top deck. "I've not got all day to wait." We saw a patent leather shoe tentatively feeling its way down the steps.

"Wait, wait!" It was Grietjie's high-pitched voice. "I'm coming as fast as I can . . ."

"*Mama mia!*" Carla leaped onto the bus, and helped the old woman down the stairs. Grietjie collapsed into her arms. Carla glared at the conductor.

128

"The downstairs is for whites only," the conductor shouted as he pressed his bell.

It was not until after lunch that Kobie found an opportunity to talk to his mother alone. Carla had refused to allow Grietjie to help with the washing-up, and insisted that she talk to Kobie on the verandah.

"Ma," Kobie said. "Ma, I want you to help me."

Grietjie's face was blank.

"Ma, who was my father?" Kobie blurted the question. There was no flicker of expression in Grietjie's yellow face. The eyes were inscrutable black discs.

"Ma, who was my father?" he asked again.

"He was a wonderful man."

"Was he a white man, Ma?"

"He was a lion among white men."

"Is he alive, Ma?"

Grietjie rose and moved into the house. "I pray he is," she said.

"It is really rather difficult not knowing whether your father is alive or dead," Hymie Ratz said irritably. "Surely you must realize that I need facts or I'm just wasting my time. Will your mother testify?"

"No, Mr. Ratz," Kobie said. "She will not."

"What is your mother's classification?"

"Her mother was a Hottentot. Her father was a Bushman. She is classified as colored."

"Well now," Hymie said, "it is essential that you should be well prepared and conversant with the procedure. You must understand what is required. I'm presenting a case to the Race Classification Board this afternoon. I can get you in."

"Yes," Kobie said. "I would like that."

"Would you care to come along, Doctor? Good. Meet me at 38 Queen Victoria Street at ten minutes to two. Don't be late."

The courtroom in the old Victorian building was small

and stuffy. The three members of the Board, all retired magistrates pleased to augment a meager pension, were ranged behind a bench in magisterial robes.

The applicant proved to be a pretty young girl of twenty. The state representative sat below the bench in the role of prosecutor. The chairman asked the girl to stand. The members of the board stared at her critically.

"She looks white enough," one member yawned.

The chairman glared at his colleague and cleared his throat. He addressed the applicant. "You carry a colored identity card?" he asked. "An objection has been lodged by someone who claims to be a friend. He states that, in fact, you are white."

I saw the girl acknowledge the chairman's address with frightened eyes. She had obviously not sought this ordeal. It seemed that everyone in the room, except perhaps Mr. Ratz and the prosecutor, wished they were elsewhere.

"Can you explain why you carry a colored card?" the chairman asked the girl.

"It has been a mistake," Hymie Ratz interjected. "She is regarded as white by all her associates, friends, and her employer. Perhaps we should ask Mr. Loots, the investigator, to explain the circumstances."

"I have a good case here," Hymie whispered to me. "Just you watch."

"This person attended a colored school in Johannesburg." Mr. Loots said. "She works as a machinist amongst colored girls. She simply took a colored card."

"Oh . . ." the chairman said. "Oh, I see . . ."

The man who had lodged the objection was called to state his case. "I was profoundly shocked to learn that this young lady had a colored card," he said.

The state attorney smirked. "Are you interested in this girl?"

The objector looked grieved and cast an appealing glance at the chairman of the board. "I am a married man with two children and very happy. This young lady is a friend of the family."

130

"I see." The state representative was sarcastic. "I have definite evidence that she works alongside colored women. She uses non-white toilets and frequents colored restrooms. She is even classified as colored by her union."

"She is classified by her union according to her identity card," Hymie Ratz interjected. "There are no white toilets on the floor where she works."

The state attorney turned to Hymie. "Why does she not go downstairs to use the white toilet, if she is white?"

"What about her father?" The chairman sounded bored.

"Her father has a white identity card." Hymie Ratz handed the card up to the chairman.

"And your mother?" The chairman addressed the girl.

"My mother is dead. She died when I was born."

"Why did you go to a colored school?"

"We were very poor. It was the closest."

Mr. Ratz interrupted again. "All her uncles and natural relatives are regarded as white."

"Call the witness,'" the chairman said wearily.

A pretty woman with two babes in arms stepped into the witness box. She was well-dressed and very white.

The state attorney was on the attack. "Is your husband white?"

The young woman looked at him reproachfully. "My husband is white. He is a cousin of Doreen." She indicated the applicant.

A succession of witnesses confirmed the impression that the girl was indeed white. It appeared that she attended white cinemas and restaurants. Her boyfriend was white. At home her friends were all white. Some of her neighbors were colored, but they regarded her as white.

A priest presented an affidavit stating that she was accepted as white in the Anglican Church. A doctor produced a certificate to say that, in his considered opinion, she was white. Hymie Ratz produced the marriage and death certificates of the applicant's late uncle.

The state attorney conceded that the evidence of the witnesses would have to be taken into account. "But we

131

cannot get away from the fact that this woman attended a colored school, that she works alongside coloreds and even uses their toilets. She must be regarded as a colored and treated accordingly."

Hymie Ratz was on his feet. "She is regarded as white by all her friends and employers. A case has been made out in terms of the Act. All I am required to do is prove that her appearance is white and that her friends are white. This I have done."

I noticed that Kobie was sweating.

The applicant had taken her stand in the witness box. Her eyes were brimming but she fought back her tears. "It is true that I work alongside colored girls," she whispered, "but they all regard me as white. My grandmother was white. As far as I know, my grandfather was white."

"So really, it is only the applicant's mother who is uncertain," the chairman said.

"That is the whole point!" The state attorney was triumphant.

The chairman looked at the girl — a long dispassionate stare. "You look white," he said. He had a further whispered discussion with his colleagues before rapping the bench.

"This Board is satisfied that this woman is white." The chairman turned to the state attorney. "Instruct the Department of the Secretary of the Interior to give her a white identity card," he said flatly.

He turned to the girl. "You may no longer use the toilets which are reserved for coloreds."

We watched the Board file out.

It was pleasant to get out into God's clean air. The ancient trees in the Public Gardens across the street were green and cool and fresh. Cars honked in the street.

"You see, it can be done," Hymie Ratz said as he walked along the pavement.

"No, Mr. Ratz, that I could not do," Kobie said. "I do not want to be white. Goodbye, Mr. Ratz."

"You know where to find me," Hymie Ratz called after us.

"I am going to tell Carla," Kobie said, turning to me.

"I agree, Kobie. Would you like me to be with you when you tell her?"

"Please, Baas Paul. Tonight."

It was a cool and quiet evening in the house on Signal Hill. The wind sighed in the stone pines. From within the house, Roberto could be heard humming himself to sleep. Carla was bent low over her mending, her face silhouetted against the pink afterglow of the sunset across the bay. In the darkening city below, lights became more numerous with each passing second.

Carla put a hand on Kobie's knee. "Times are not easy for us and for Roberto, no?"

"Things have not been easy, but they are all right now," Kobie said.

Carla smiled and moved across to sit by him on the bench, resting her head on his shoulder. She slid her hand inside his shirt and placed it over his heart.

"In Italy we know about politicians," she said. "Some people farm with cows, some with sheep, and others with pigs. Politicians farm with people . . . feed them a little, starve them a little, move them a little, as long as they bring the politician the best profit. We have learned to live with them from the beginning of time. Politicians in the church, politicians outside the church, always they live on the people for their own benefit. Some seem good, some are bad. Some they kill, others they put in prison. Some they crucify. But the people, the real people, they go on! They live, they love, they die. It is no matter to us that there are men in your country that say, he is white, he is brown, he is black, he is English, he is Afrikaner, he is Catholic, he is Jew." Carla tapped her fingers on Kobie's chest, enumerating the categories. "It is here, what is in the heart, that matters. Your heart is good, my Kobie, my heart is good, our child's

133

heart is good. It is we who do not wish to lie, cheat, and murder, who have no need to be afraid. It is the politicians who must worry. They must worry when they think of that frog Mussolini. Poof! Look at him! The people hung him up by his feet!"

I saw that Kobie was speechless with emotion.

Carla continued. "If Roberto must go to another school, he goes to another school. If they say we must move to another place, we move to another place. Our Roberto can hold his own with any man, high or low. We live, we are strong, and we love." She smiled up at Kobie. "I look at the pictures of political men in the newspaper. I know in my heart that they have never made love, not as we make love!"

She turned and took his face between her hands. "The world is a good place as long as we are together, my Kobie." His tears trickled through her fingers. "That would be the only reason for tears — if we were not together."

But, as luck would have it, fate granted a reprieve. Gammatjie owned a house in District VI, which hadn't yet been re-zoned white. The old Malay who rented the premises was found dead in his bed. Gammatjie and Fatima, it was decided, would live on the ground floor. Kobie and Carla would rent the upstairs apartment. The sentence of banishment to the bleak new colored townships on the windswept wastes of the Cape Flats was at least suspended.

19

I shall always remember that young man. I saw him only once, and then very briefly. I have never known his name. But over the years, at the most unaccountable times, the swirling mists of memory suddenly clear to reveal his face. Sometimes I feel a genuine sympathy, not untinged with mirth, but more often I experience a depressing sense of futility. Rather as a head embossed on a coin represents a realm, so has the face of that young man come to symbolize the quality of my life.

I cannot remember whether it was a drug, an instrument, or a medical journal I needed that afternoon. But at approximately three o'clock I drove to what I had come to think of as "Ma Hackstone's house." It was the hour when the servants retired for siesta, and Nanny took Jeremy walking in the park.

A fine autumn day it was, with the occasional brown oak leaf drifting gently to the lawn. A green M.G. was parked in the drive. The house was quiet, and I fetched whatever it was I needed from my study. As I was about to leave, I decided to use the upstairs toilet. I so wish I had not.

But there they were. What does a man do when confronted with the spectacle of his wife copulating with a stranger in his bed? Does he turn and leave? Does he say,

"Excuse me, please continue"? Or does he grab the nearest blunt object and commit a bloody murder? I know that I stood at the door and said, "Bloody hell!"

He whipped over like a scalded cat and stood loose-mouthed and scared stiff, clutching the corner of the sheet to his belly. I swear Fiona's eyes were about to pop out of her head as she rested on her elbows in the bed.

Time froze, and that young man's face made an indelible imprint on my mind. Perhaps the striking of the clock in the hall broke the spell. He turned then, dragging the bedclothes off Fiona in his urgency. She wrenched them back to cover her nakedness.

He cursed as he dressed — shorts, shirt, trousers. Then he came at me barefooted, carrying shoes, jacket, and tie. I swung at him. "You bastard!" I yelled.

He ducked and rushed past me, taking the stairs three at a time. I heard the front door bang and the roar of the M.G. in the drive.

Fiona was pulling on a robe when I returned.

"What the hell are you doing here?" She glared at me in the mirror as she ran a comb through her mussed hair.

"I might ask the same of you," I said.

"Hell," she retorted. "Hell!" She flung the comb on the dressing table, scattering trinkets onto the floor. "What a bloody fool I feel!"

"Fiona, we can't go on like this."

She looked at me directly then. "I can, and I intend to."

"Oh no, you won't," I said. "I'll give you the option of divorcing me, but believe me, if you don't, I shall divorce you."

"You will not. What do you take me for, a fool? Do you think I don't know about you?"

"What about me?"

"About you and that Italian bint married to that colored."

"What about Carla?"

"Carla, is it? Oh now it's Carla, is it?"

136

She lit a cigarette. "I've had you watched. Your car parked on Signal Hill all hours of the day and night. And usually when he's out."

"That's a lie."

"Not according to the agency, it isn't."

"You have no proof."

"Proof! Proof! Proof of what? Don't you know the law in your own bloody country? She is married to a colored and registered as a colored, isn't she?" Fiona lifted triumphant eyebrows.

"You must be mad!"

She smiled. "Sleep on it, Ducky. I can see the headlines — 'Society doctor charged under Immorality Act.'"

I was speechless with horror.

'No, Paul, darling, I like it this way. Do as you like, but don't crowd me — understand?"

It was then I built a house in Constantia. I could no longer stand the humiliation of living in Ma Hackstone's damned house. At least I would have decent private quarters under the roof of our continuing marriage charade.

20

Tertius le Bois . . . Dr. Tertius le Bois . . . How had I managed to tolerate that ridiculous little bastard all these years? It must be damn near twenty years!

He came at a time of ferment, a time when the first alarming signs of the new order were wafting across the land like the scent of lion among buck. The Afrikaner majority in Parliament was as yet slender.

"The colored people must be removed from the voters' roll," the prime minister announced. "Apartheid is our policy."

Three times the High Court ruled the proposal unconstitutional.

"Does the dove couple with the starling?" Dominee Verwyt cried from the pulpit. "Is the Afrikaner to be controlled by an act of English liberalism perpetrated in 1909?"

The constitutional obstacle was overcome by appointing enough loyal senators to secure the required two-thirds majority in a combined sitting of both Houses.

Uncle Gert was indignant. "So the bastards have done it again, and all in the name of Afrikanerdom!" He thumped his chest with the flat of his hand. "Must I, Gert Cilliers, as a white man, stand accused of breaking my solemn pledge to the Cape Colored people?"

"I would be careful where you say that, Gert," my mother cautioned.

Fiona joined the Black Sash movement, a select band of cultured, intelligent women of conscience who donned black sashes and stood on streetcorners with heads bowed in solemn mourning for the Constitution.

Ernie Hackstone had lost his monopoly in scrap iron, the new apartheid laws were complicating the stevedoring business, and real estate was down. "Pure Nazism," Ernie said.

"I'm keeping my British passport," Ma Hackstone announced.

"We have simply got to expand," Reggie Bentwhistle said. "Now this chap le Bois wants to join us. More and more of these Afrikaners are moving into our area. This chap seems to have influence in the right circles. If you can't beat 'em, join 'em, what? Got to move with the times, old boy."

Tertius le Bois, graduate of the new Afrikaans Medical School in Pretoria, was a chunky little man who looked and moved as if made of India rubber. Large, unblinking, pale blue eyes stared watchfully through round, gold-rimmed spectacles. Even at that first encounter, I sensed a passive aggression in Tertius le Bois. With silent efficiency he installed himself in our office suite. On the wall behind his desk a life-size portrait of Adolph Hitler glowered.

"I wish you to meet some of my friends," Tertius announced to me one day. Will you come to my house on Saturday night?"

"Does that include my wife?" I enquired.

"No," he said. "This is for men alone."

"Will Dr. Bentwhistle be coming too?"

"No, he came last night," Tertius said flatly.

Three Mercedes Benz cars were parked outside the le Bois residence in the new Afrikaner suburb. The name "Outspan" pricked out in glass reflectors hung on a gate fashioned from two large red-painted wagon wheels. The mounted horns of a variety of antelope adorned the porch.

Martha le Bois, a large, fresh-complexioned woman rendered larger by a pink crepe de chine frock, answered the door. Her feet bulged painfully in high-heeled, patent leather shoes. She did not smile.

"Come in, Doctor," she said.

A German shepherd dog slunk growling into the hall. Martha le Bois kicked at it. "*Voetsek*, Izan!" The dog cringed away. I followed Martha into the drawing room, which was Spanish style, plastered in lime green. A flight of six pink plaster seagulls swooped down one wall. The whole house, which posterity would probably date as "Lebanese 1940," was furnished with massively uncomfortable "pioneer" pieces which seemed just a little self-conscious.

Tertius le Bois detached himself from a group of men at the far end of the room and came to meet me.

"Welcome to my house," he said. "Let me present you to my friends."

They stood in a row, gravely acknowledging my introduction.

"Our mayor in Pretoria, Meneer Staltz; my attorney Meneer Steyn; and Meneer Binnewald who is the richest farmer in the Western Transvaal."

Solemnly they shook my hand. "How goes it?" each asked. How I wish I had told them then; but I knew the drill.

"Can't complain," I said.

"You speak very good Afrikaans for an Englishman," Meneer Binnewald said.

"But I'm not English."

"But that is really wonderful, man," Meener Steyn said. "When I first saw you I thought you looked just like one."

What the hell does one say, I thought.

Meneer Steyn continued. "As a brother Afrikaner, you will appreciate how important it is for people to be able to consult a doctor who speaks their own language."

"Very true," I conceded.

"The Senator Dominee Verwyt wrote and told me about you," Meneer Staltz confided. "He wrote to say he had known your family a long time."

"Really!" Meneer Binnewald feigned surprise. "Now that is a truly great Afrikaner. There are many who believe that one day the Dominee Verwyt will be our next prime minister."

"Dominee Verwyt and my mother grew up together," I said.

"My wife is a cousin of Dominee Verwyt's wife," Meneer Staltz said with obvious pride.

"Oh, really?" I said.

With traditional enthusiasm Tertius le Bois poured the brandy. Later Martha le Bois joined us for the meal of roast mutton.

They spoke of preparations for their annual camping holiday by the sea. Last year it had been screamingly funny when Tertius le Bois poured a bucket of cold water over someone who was very drunk.

The episode reminded Martha of the time when Mrs. Steyn was sitting in the shallows and a sudden big wave displaced her bathing costume while the menfolk were fishing nearby.

"They were all married men," Martha said defiantly, "and any man who looked should have been ashamed of himself."

There was milk tart for dessert. "You must have more," Meneer Steyn told me. "Martha's milk tart is the best. Is that not so, Martha?"

"Yes," she said. "It is the best."

Dinner over, Martha disappeared once again.

"You will find," Meneer Binnewald confided to me over more brandy, "that we are well organized. I am chairman of the Nationalist Party in my district in the Transvaal. We had an old doctor up there called Jacobson — a Jew. Now that we are organized and have our own man, he sees very few white patients. We must look after our own, is it not so?

141

I have told Tertius that if he plays his cards right, there is a fortune to be made here."

"Indeed," I said, "indeed."

Binnewald became indulgent. "There is a new nation of Afrikaners aware of their heritage but also aware of their future. The *volkswil* has manifested itself to keep the blacks in their place and foster our interests. In big things and in small, the Afrikaner must come first. This is the country of the Afrikaner, is it not?"

Le Bois entered the discussion. "Our struggle must be fought everywhere. Why, right here in this hospital I have had to fight to get the nurses to write reports in Afrikaans. Why should I, an Afrikaner, have to read a report on an Afrikaner patient, written in English? It's disgraceful! They say they don't know the Afrikaans terms because they took their training in English. So I wrote to Pretoria for a dictionary of the new terms, and since then I have torn up three reports written in English."

"Did you read what the Archbishop of Canterbury wrote in the English newspapers this morning?" Meneer Steyn was trying to change the subject.

"No, I've not seen the papers," I said.

"Well, he writes that we Afrikaners are not Christian in our apartheid policy. These English are so ignorant and so decadent. He has the temerity to quote the Word in support of his ideas. Does the Word not say 'Be ye separate'? Little does he know that such statements only make the flame of Afrikanerdom burn brighter!"

"I see what you mean," I said.

I should have known then that Tertius le Bois was a Broederbond watchdog.

What crazy, desperate years those were! Ironic years when the initiators of apartheid, aware of its fallacy, fortified themselves and those they had deluded with ever greater legislative lunacy.

South Africa left the British Commonwealth. The refer-

142

endum on the republic issue was carried by the narrowest of margins.

Blood transfusions across the color bar became illegal. A black ambulance could not pick up a white casualty.

At his Anglican Church school, the rugby matches my son Jeremy played against Afrikaans schools were like a tableau of the Boer War.

South Africa was kicked out of the United Nations. Dominee Verwyt was indignant. "Do we interfere in the internal affairs of other nations?" he ranted.

South Africa was excluded from participation in international sport. "It is just because they know we are the best," the Dominee rationalized. "We don't need them."

Years of riots in Durban, riots in Port Elizabeth, riots in Johannesburg, riots in Cape Town. Hangings, arrests, and white university students protesting educational apartheid clubbed into submission by police on the steps of St. George's Anglican Cathedral.

Years when the buying and selling went on as before and the giant finance houses built ever bigger buildings. Gold, diamonds, uranium, wool, fruit, and maize flowed out. The percentages were collected, and the money flowed in.

Years when thousands of books, films, periodicals — anything which might expose the public to critical outside thought — were censored or banned, and the opposition press was muzzled by threats of closure.

Years when parliamentary opposition, cowed by coercive laws and aware that the point of no return had been passed, was reduced to a token, carping about anything but the main issue.

Years when the new prime minister formulated an "outward policy" towards the rest of Africa. Dominee Verwyt was incensed, and his newspaper *Die Voorslag*, representative of the "purified Nationalists," published a "humiliating" picture of the prime minister dining between two black women.

That was the year when a Sicilian usher stabbed Dominee

143

Verwyt to death in the Senate. The Sicilian, it was said, was of unsound mind and could not stand trial. "Sanest man in the land," Uncle Gert growled. And the prime minister was constrained to unveil three stone plinths, commemorating the Afrikaner men, women, and children who had perished in English concentration camps in the Boer War.

Those were years when Kobie's taxi business thrived. Somehow he had collected a following of wealthy dowagers, many of them my patients. In return for deferential service and a kindly ear for the problems of their affluent loneliness, the tips far exceeded the fare. "May I have an appointment for three o'clock, Doctor? You see, that is the time I have Mr. September." They called themselves the September Club.

Years when Kobie September became the uncrowned king of District VI — arbiter in disputes, champion in trouble, benefactor in sickness and poverty, avenger of the persecuted and terror of the evil. He refused nomination for the newly constituted Council for Cape Colored Affairs while remaining consultant to the slightly embarrassed members of this impotent government gesture to the cult of apartheid. He was Chairman of the Cape Colored Boys' Brigade, president of the Cape Colored Rugby Association, president of the Cape Colored Cricket Association, member of the Cape Colored Branch of the Red Cross Society. Mr. September . . . he neither complained nor explained. Kobie September walked alone.

Years when Belle Fleur came into its own, and the only regret the wine merchants voiced was that they could not get more of it. A year when Aunt Hannah Cilliers died, and my mother retired from teaching and returned to Fleur to keep house for Uncle Gert.

It was inevitable, I suppose, that Tertius le Bois and I would clash. How I grew to hate those morning tea sessions in the hospital! Dr. Gerhardus Krag, the medical superintendent, was always there. His attendance, as he frequently stated, was based on a determination to know everything that went on in his hospital. Dr. Vlakman, fat and bald, was a good doctor who did his work and kept his mouth shut. Dr. Gylwater, an ugly little chap, was tormented by an agonizing curiosity about everybody and everything.

"So the convent has asked if their children may join our children at rugby practice," Dr. Gylwater said.

"I believe so," Dr. Vlakman replied. "They have only nine little boys . . . not enough to form a team."

"What is your feeling?" Dr. Gylwater bit furiously at a match, spitting splinters.

Dr. Vlakman patted his abdomen and momentarily lifted hooded eyes. "Who am I, a simple Afrikaner, to give an expression on such important matters?"

"Good morning, Tertius." Reggie Bentwhistle was on his feet vacating his chair at the head of the table. Tertius le Bois stood unblinking at the door.

"Come and sit down, Tertius." Reggie wrinkled his nose. "May I get you some tea?"

Without comment Tertius le Bois took his seat at the head of the table.

"We were just discussing a problem." Dr. Gylwater started on a new match. "The convent wants their pupils to practice rugby with our children."

Tertius gave his ruling. "The matter has been dealt with by the school board. This is a Calvinist country. If parents wish their children to play rugby, they know where to send them."

"That sounds reasonable." Reggie Bentwhistle served the tea.

Dr. Krag passed Tertius a typed sheet. "A colored doctor has put in an application to treat his colored patients in our colored section."

"He can send them in if he likes" — Tertius le Bois passed the letter back — "but we will take them over on admission."

145

Dr. Gylwater was down to his last match. "What would happen if this colored doctor had to give an order to a white nurse?"

"Very awkward," Reggie Bentwhistle conceded.

To me there was something horribly simian about the room. Everyone was uneasy, nervous, alert for any opportunity for personal advantage or sign of danger — always on guard, fidgeting, humorless, greedy, vicious. Disloyal to anything and everything, only clinging together because cohesion, distasteful as it was, presented the optimum advantage under the circumstances.

"What utter rubbish," I snapped. "You all constantly grumble about the honorary work you do for the coloreds. If this colored doctor is an accredited doctor and wishes to treat his patients, why should he not do so?"

"It is against the traditional way of life." Dr. Gylwater said.

"The provincial ordinance makes no provision for such an application," Dr. Krag said. "I shall refer it to head office."

Tertius le Bois was on his feet. "I am chairman of the Medical Committee. No colored is going to give an order to a white nurse in this hospital." He addressed me directly. "People who do not like the law in this country are free to leave."

Reggie Bentwhistle cast me a look of frantic disapproval. "Oh Tertius, Tertius . . ." He followed le Bois into the passage. "Tertius, about the matter of this application . . ."

Dr. Vlakman rubbed his stomach and burped.

I made an enemy of our partner Tertius le Bois that day.

Politics in the morning, politics in the evening, and politics at Fiona's eternal little "dins." All those years when my work was occupational therapy for me, and Kobie's house in District VI my only refuge.

146

21

That last Friday!

The minutest details will always be with me. It was the last day I saw Kobie.

I dropped in to see Carla at her store on my way to the hospital in the late afternoon. Carla's Cash Store, as she called it, was located in what had been the old carriageway of Gammatjie's house in District VI. Kobie had fitted a display window on the pavement and bricked up the back. Into this confined space Carla, with shrewd attention to the needs of her exclusively colored clientele, had crammed every conceivable variety of merchandise ranging from bolts of linen and every kind of foodstuff, to lavatory seats and bicycle bells. Carla and her customers treated each other with mutual respect and hearty friendliness. Accordingly, Carla's Cash Store became a place where confidences were safe, a refuge in times of trouble, and, despite its name, a place where credit could be obtained for almost anything. And it was credit without interest. This last principle was highly valued in a community where ready cash was rare, and exigency a constant dread. In consequence, any debtor who failed to honor his commitment faced the wrath and reprisal of the whole community. On this basis Carla had no bad debts, and many friends.

It was almost closing time. The shop was deserted except for one large man in white overalls.

"Paulie, hullo," Carla greeted me from behind the counter. "This is Mr. Badoupolos who travels for the sweet factory . . . Meet Dr. Pendrake."

"A lovely day, sir." Mr. Badoupolos shook my hand.

"It's spring!" Carla flung up her hands. "Last time you were here it was winter. Your mint toffees sold very well. The people thought they helped for colds. Have you any more, Mr. Badoupolos?"

"Of course, of course." Mr. Badoupolos wrote down the order.

"How is your wife?" Carla asked him.

The Greek spread his arms wide and beamed. "She is so happy now. I was right to come to Cape Town. This is a good place. I cannot believe we were so unhappy."

"Unhappy?" I said. "Why were you so unhappy?"

Mr. Badoupolos wrinkled his nose. "You ask me why we were unhappy?" He looked at me searchingly. "Have you ever been out of Cape Town, doctor?"

"Why yes, of course."

"Beyond the mountains?"

"Well, yes," I smiled, "why do you ask?"

"Because out there it is hell . . . as different as night from day, as light from darkness." He passed the order form for Carla to sign.

"How do you mean?"

"It is not an easy story to tell."

"Tell the doctor," Carla said.

Mr. Badoupolos folded his arms on the counter. "Two years ago I am in Athens. I am a graduate of the business school in Salonica. I have written a book, and am thirty-five years old. A job is offered in Massachusetts, but I read the brochures of the South African Immigration and I think this country looks good. I apply, and I get a job in Pretoria, a good job."

148

"Good for you," I said.

"Doctor, you have heard as yet nothing." He turned down the corners of his mouth. "It is known to me that to learn Afrikaans is very desirable. So I buy Afrikaans books, and tapes, and records. From the first day they laugh at me when I try to speak Afrikaans. They call me a dirty Greek. They say I should go back to Greece. They call me a Catholic." His voice was high-pitched with incredulity. "I am Greek Orthodox!"

"It was not easy for him, believe me," Carla said to me.

"Greeks, they say, are only good for running dirty cafes. Jobs like mine, they say, are reserved for Afrikaner people. It was impossible. I wanted to go home to Greece but" — Mr. Badoupolos shook his head — "I fell in love with an Afrikaner girl who became my wife. So I asked the company for a transfer to a mine in the Namib Desert. Perhaps there, if I was in charge of the office, it would be better. But it was no better. My wife, too, was excluded. Afrikaner children called her names and threw stones at her in the streets."

"Shameful," I said.

Badoupolos shrugged. "I tore up my books, broke my records, and cut my tapes up with scissors . . . and we left for Cape Town. Now I sell sweets and we are happy."

"I am so glad," I said.

"It is over now," Mr. Badoupolos smiled ruefully. "My wife and I are happy — poor but happy. Next month our child will be born." He pointed north. "Out there over the mountains it is sour with hate. We save our money. If the hatred comes over the mountains, we take our child and go back to Greece."

"Who will bring me mint toffee?" Carla smiled. "Please stay."

Badoupolos kissed her hand. "Bless you, Missus Carla," he said. "Bless you. Goodbye, doctor."

"What a bloody shame!" I said as he left.

149

Carla shrugged. "It is an old story, Paulie." She was removing her smock. "Have you time to drive me to church?"

I helped her switch out the lights and padlock the shop. She took my arm. There was a warm breath of spring in the street. The sun setting across the bay gilded the dilapidated facades of the Victorian houses. A colored flower seller, squatting by her bucket on the pavement, offered a bouquet of daisies. "A present for you, Missus Carla."

Carla patted the toothless cheek. "Thank you, Katie."

"God bless, Missus Carla."

In the car Carla said, "Today is a very special day for me, Paulie. It is the anniversary of my Day of Resolutions."

For the first time, Carla confessed to me how she really felt about what her life with Kobie had become.

"As this beautiful land has been changed by those awful men, falsely in the name of God, my love for it has changed to sorrow, and then to hate, Paulie." She shuddered as she very quietly gave voice to her fears.

She told me of her three resolutions before Holy Mary, Mother of God: Never again to own a house in this land; never to conceive another child until she and Kobie were safely beyond South African shores; and to scrimp and save and bend every effort toward the day when they could go to a new life in Rome.

Her eyes were glistening with tears when I left her on the steps of the cathedral and hurried to my duties at the hospital.

The intern met me at the door of the Casualty Department. He was sweating and his green gown was stained with blood. There was mild reproach in his tone.

"We have been beeping you, sir."

"I came as soon as I could," I said.

Friday night and payday! The stench of unwashed bodies, cheap wine, and the oddly sweet reek of spilt blood enveloped me. How familiar I was with this scene! Friday night after Friday night in every hospital throughout the land. Was this the product of poverty, deprivation of political rights, or the maniacal depravity that urban over-crowding brings? Would I, under similar circumstance, behave this way?

The nursing sister in charge was undoing the straps restraining a patient whose lacerated scalp the intern had just stitched. The patient, a drunken colored woman clad in a filthy blood-stained shirt, swore and kicked out at the nurse. Unable to stand, she flopped to the floor and vomited, wiping her mouth with the back of her hand.

In a far corner a young colored youth in tight red slacks and high-heeled boots sat softly moaning. His eyes were bandaged. "Stab wound," the intern said. "The eye will have to come out. I've telephoned the ophthalmologist."

On the steel drip tray of the sluice lay the body of a child under a towel. I lifted the towel. The abdomen of the child was ripped across, the guts macerated, the liver a mess. Blood dripped into the sink. "The father, I gather," the intern said.

"There is a patient I want you to see, sir." The intern walked ahead.

We crossed the lobby to where a young girl huddled miserably on a bench, clutching a blood-soaked pillow to her chest. She was gray with shock. Two relatives supported the girl into the examination room. I eased the pillow away gently. The breasts were a gory mess, both nipples gone.

An older woman standing at the door said, "They did it with a sickle. She was on her way home from the factory. They took her money."

"Get some O positive blood going as soon as you can," I told the intern. "She is too shocked to touch."

The intern led me to another patient.

The boy was about ten years old. A woman stood sobbing near the stretcher. The child's eyes were wild with terror.

151

Six inches of bicycle spoke protruded from the base of his neck. The bright steel oscillated like a metronome with each pulse beat.

"He is such a good child," the mother sobbed.

"We shall have to explore that neck," I said to the intern. "Please notify the operating theater."

"They will be ready in fifteen minutes, sir."

"Call me when you're ready," I said. "I shall be on B floor." I hurried to the white section.

Sister van der Boewe sat slumped at her desk in the duty room. She was one of the "new" ones — truculent, militantly Afrikaans and determined to show it by speaking only Afrikaans.

"*Goeie naand*, Sister," I said.

The woman did not reply. Instead she looked pointedly at her watch, closed the report book on her desk, and flung down her pen. "All this writing makes a person sick," she said. She sighed resignedly. "I'm off duty at seven."

"I'd like to see Mrs. Gerber. She is being transferred to the renal unit tomorrow."

Sister van der Boewe smirked, lurched to her feet, and strolled ahead of me down the hall.

I found old Mrs. Gerber in tears. She sat in bed gently mopping her eyes with a sodden handkerchief.

"What on earth is the matter?" I asked.

Sister van der Boewe turned down the corners of her mouth and shrugged.

"There now," I said, putting an arm round the old lady's shoulder. "I shall come and visit you regularly. You won't be alone. You will be well looked after. Now don't cry. Just be thankful we have an opportunity to help you."

The old lady reached out and took my hand. She did not look up. "I'm not going," she whimpered.

"But Mrs. Gerber, you need treatment. Dr. Barwell is the best man in the country. He has written widely on the subject. He is a recognized authority, and he is very nice."

Mrs. Gerber looked at me beseechingly. "I cannot go."

152

She clutched my hand. "Please understand, doctor, it is not so much my wish. I want to get better. But Dr. le Bois was here this afternoon. He reminded me that it is my duty to go to a specialist who sits in the same church. He told me to ask you to send me to Dr. van Erwen. He is one of our people, you see, Dr. Pendrake. Dr. le Bois says that he is better than anyone else." Mrs. Gerber broke down and sobbed uncontrollably.

Sister van der Boewe was smirking again. I looked at the sobbing old lady on the bed. "Of course, my dear, I can arrange that for you. Now, don't worry. I'll write up something for you to sleep tonight."

"Will you, doctor? Ag, but you are always so good to me. You do understand how it is, don't you doctor?"

"Of course I do, Mrs. Gerber."

I followed Sister van der Boewe to the duty room. She drew a form from a pigeonhole and slapped it on the desk. "You will probably want to cancel the transfer sheet for tomorrow, doctor."

At that moment the operating room nurse came up briskly. "We are ready, sir. You are wanted on the telephone. It sounds urgent."

It was Kobie's voice. "Baas Paul! Is that you? It's Carla . . . She's hurt, Baas Paul . . . They got her in the street . . . Please come, Baas Paul . . . Please . . ."

"Ask Dr. Noordstrom to take over," I called to the intern. "Something urgent has come up. I must go at once." I ran down the corridor and out of the hospital on my way to District VI.

By the time I got there, Carla had calmed down somewhat, although there was still evidence of her brush with death in her eyes and in her hysterical voice. She was lying on her bed, hair disheveled, dress torn, left ankle painfully swollen and beginning to turn blue. Kobie, Roberto, and even Gammatjie were no less upset than the victim herself.

By the time I had ascertained that there were no serious

153

injuries and had given Carla an injection of morphia, tetanus toxoid, and penicillin, their fear was transformed to anger and hatred.

"It was Red Fink," growled Kobie through clenched teeth. "Red Fink and his gang of thugs with their killer dogs. Only last week I threw him out of Carla's shop."

Red Fink, a Negro half-breed with red fuzzy hair, was the leader of a gang of youths, traffickers in illicit liquor and drugs, and experts at extortion. They terrorized the colored townships. Their dogs were vicious and superbly trained.

As I listened I lived Carla's horror . . .

It was that strange hour of evening respite when the city-dweller is either at home recovering from the day or preparing for the night, and the streets beyond the brightly lit center of town are virtually deserted.

Carla first noticed Red Fink at the corner of Roeland and Buitenkant Streets, a block or so from the cathedral where she had gone to pray. The green, amber, and red of the changing traffic lights reflected weirdly on his red Afro fuzz and waxen face. The dog sitting at his feet watched her with pricked ears. A car, traveling fast, hissed towards de Waal Drive.

Carla turned into Buitenkant Street. She glanced over her shoulder. The man with the dog was moving down the opposite pavement. The dog was still watching her. She was aware of the sound of footsteps echoing through the mist. She felt the taste of fear in her mouth. She turned her head again. It was Fink, all right.

The lights of a petrol station glared ahead. She would telephone Kobie to come and fetch her. A black attendant was filling the tank of a car.

Carla took a ten-cent coin from her bag. "Can you help me? I wish to telephone, please."

The black man did not look up. "Office is closed," he said.

Carla noted that Red Fink and his dog had stopped on the other side of the street. "Please, have you not got the key?"

The attendant was not interested. He sauntered round to the driver. He took the customer's money and clipped out the change from a bag at his waist. Carla could feel her heart pumping in her throat. She approached the driver of the car.

"Please," she said, "can you give me a lift home?"

"Where do you live?"

"Just two block down in District VI . . . de Korte Street."

"Are you colored?"

Carla hesitated a moment. "Yes, I am colored."

There was fear and indignation on the little man's face. "You should be locked up!" he said, starting the engine. "Next thing, I'm in for the Immorality Act. If I had the time, I'd have you arrested." The car leapt forward with a squeal of tires. The black attendant sauntered into the garage and sat down on a box, picking his nose.

Carla decided to pull herself together. She would proceed down Buitenkant Street and head for the police station. At the police station they all knew Kobie. The police knew the problem. They would take her home. She could not resist glancing over her shoulder. Red Fink and his dog were moving too. Carla resisted the impulse to break into a run.

A man who looked like a dockworker came towards her, walking fast. He carried a food tin, and wore a black peaked cap.

"Please, can you help me?" Carla said.

The man glanced at her, sidestepped and hurried into the mist. Across the road, by the warehouse, Red Fink had stopped to light a cigarette. The mongrel sat at his feet peering at Carla. The light of the police station gleamed hopefully through the mist. She stopped in her tracks. At the corner a man with a black Alsatian at his feet leaned against the lamp post, blocking her path. The man came slowly toward her. Carla ran into the road. A car looming through the mist braked, honked, and drove on. She was running now. The mist was swirling round the buildings. Another car passed down Buitenkant Street. Carla called after it, waving her arms. The red taillights melted into the mist. She knew then that the night had been planned.

How often had Kobie told her of these organized attacks which left bleeding corpses in the street. She must get home. She crossed the road and ran into Commercial Street. It was dark and deserted, yawning like a chasm between the buildings. The men with the dogs followed her, one dog yelping softly now, the other grunting against its leash.

Carla's heel caught in a crevice in the pavement. She ran on blindly, leaving her shoe behind. Silently she prayed. Please, Mother of God, send my husband and my son back to Rome!

Now suddenly the blackness of the street was lit up. To Carla's disturbed imagination, this was the great light of Judgment Day. Through the lights, she saw another man with a dog approaching from the front. The dog's coat was shaggy with black and white markings.

So they had cornered her! This was to be the place of her death. They would maim her. They would kill her for they feared her husband. They called Kobie "the soldier." They thought he was an informer to the police.

She ran on. The car was beside her, moving slowly now, its great cream wing almost next to her thigh, forcing her into the wall. She stumbled on. The man ahead stopped in his tracks, jerking the dog by its chain. Carla would not look at the car. This car would take her body and dump it into the sea. A stone on the pavement cut into her stockinged foot. The pain seared up her leg. She could not go on. She flattened herself against the wall. The car door was opening.

"No!" she screamed.

"Mama! What on earth?" It was the voice of her son. Carla screamed again. "They're going to kill me!" She felt herself being dragged into the car. Roberto accelerated up the street. The man with the dog was running. Finally he jumped for his life.

"She's sleeping now." Roberto came back into the living room where we were talking it over. His face was drawn with anxiety.

"We've got to get her out of here," he said to his father. "It's not safe. They'll try again, and maybe we won't be so lucky next time."

Kobie looked at his son, his face still twisted in anger.

"We've all got to get away," Roberto went on. "There's nothing here for any of us. They don't want coloreds in their schools or their churches or their so-called universities . . . We can't learn, we can't get decent jobs, we can't even enjoy ourselves. They're even going to push us out of this slum, out to the Flats. There's nothing for us but fear and death. We've got to get Ma home to Italy."

Kobie looked at him and shook his head. "This is home, Roberto. South Africa is home; and the colored people are the real South Africans. My mother was half Bushman. We built this country brick by brick with the white men. They have given us their blood and we have given them ours.

"In the war, I traveled and I fought for this country. These Afrikaners in power amount to nothing. They have values which the whole world, even the Germans, despise. They cannot last for long. Once these people in power slip, they'll slip all the way. Believe me, when I was your age, it was even tougher than it is now. It was tougher for me, and I haven't done too badly."

Kobie kept his eyes on his son. "Not all white men are bad, Roberto. I have some wonderful white friends. Not all colored men are good. The time will come when men who are men will be able to restore sanity to this great land."

"Pa, where are these white men who are your friends? What is friendship? What did even your Dr. Paul do when you were being shunted from pillar to post?"

157

Kobie was on his feet. His face was fierce. "Hold your tongue, Roberto. Baas Paul is our friend and a guest in our house." He towered over his son.

"Take it easy, Kobie," I said.

He drew a deep breath, controlling himself with great effort.

"Almost every day, Roberto, I drive foreign visitors — British, American, German, all sorts — in my taxi. Some think I am white; some recognize me as colored; all think that I am of no account because I am a taxi driver, and they are far from home — so they speak from their hearts. I know it helps them somehow. Whatever they say I listen, and I learn a lot.

"Where would you go, Roberto? To Britain? Do you know that they have racial problems too? What makes you think the British people would accept you? Would you go to America, where the dollar is God? Where everything — even the smells of their bodies and the functions of their women — is dragged through the marketplace? Do you think the white men there are any different? At least the white men who settled here didn't exterminate the natives and banish the rest to reserves. Here, at least until recently, we've lived in peace with the black people. How do you think the Americans would act if they were outnumbered five to one by blacks or Indians?"

"Oh, pa . . ."

"Roberto, a Jewish newspaperman came here from America to write an article about this country, and he gave me a lecture about the evils of apartheid when I was driving him to the airport. Roberto, if you ever think about marrying a Jewish girl, then you'll learn about apartheid — the oldest apartheid in the world.

"Would you go to Italy, Roberto? Italy was once in the grip of Mussolini, and your mother's family was almost wiped out before the country came to its senses. Do you think that South Africa is the only country to have been torn apart by its government?"

158

"No, but . . ."

"Or would you go to a black country, and have your throat cut because you are three-quarters white? Do you know what it is to be a man without a country, Roberto?"

"Of course, pa, but . . ."

"Do you know the law, Roberto? Do you know that any man who is being difficult here may be locked up without trial? Do you think it is only coloreds who suffer? Decent white men also have families. They are no more free than we are. They, too, can only wait."

Kobie was pulling on a windbreaker. "Roberto, if I must leave this country, I shall go because I want to go. I will not run away."

"Yes, Pa."

"I want you to open your mother's shop tomorrow morning. My car needs servicing. I'll take yours."

"Where are you going?"

"I am going to find Red Fink."

"For God's sake, Kobie!" I said. "Leave it to the police."

He looked at me levelly. "This is my war, Baas Paul . . . mine and mine alone."

"The Imam may be able to help you," Gammatjie said quietly. "An eye for an eye, and a tooth for a tooth."

"Be careful, Pa," Roberto called as Kobie banged down the stairs.

We heard the big Dodge roar down the street.

22

They came for me in the night.

I woke to the insistent clamor of the doorbell pealing through the house. Bemused with sleep, I switched on the bedside lamp and looked at my watch. It was 2:15. I stumbled out of bed and groped for a robe. There was a hammering at the front door. The beam of a powerful flashlight pierced the window of my bedroom. I shaded my eyes against the glare.

"Open up! Police!" a voice called from the garden. The flashlight went out. Our corgi was barking frantically. There was a yelp, and the barking stopped. I ran down the passage barefoot. The drive was bright in the headlights of parked vehicles. I wrenched at the latch of the door. My pulse was hammering in my head.

Three men stood on the porch — a uniformed policeman and two civilians. The policeman's hand was on his holster.

"You are under arrest," one of the plainclothesmen said.

"What on earth for?" I blurted out.

"Never mind that." The policeman was frisking me for weapons.

"But this is ridiculous!"

"Bureau of State Security," the policeman said.

"Oh my God!" Fiona was coming down the stairs. There were curlers in her hair. She look terrified. "I've done nothing at all," she cried hysterically.

"We're not concerned with you, madam," the plain-clothesman said. He turned to me. "You had better come with me and put your clothes on." He turned to his colleagues. "Search the house," he ordered.

Three more men came through the door. An Alsatian dog strained at a leash. I saw Stompie Lategan then. He was in uniform, gold braid on his epaulets and on the peak of his cap. He wore his campaign ribbons. How old he looked. The hair at his temples was gray. The scar on the left cheek of his deeply lined face looked livid.

I moved towards him, extending my hand. His eyes were like gimlets, willing me to silence. My greeting froze on my lips. He gave no sign of recognition.

"I've done nothing wrong," Fiona wheedled. "Nothing at all. I joined the Black Sash once, but I'm no longer a member. I know nothing about all this."

"Go to your bedroom, madam," a policeman said.

They were rummaging through my study, wrenching at the drawers of my desk. I heard wood splinter. "I have the keys," I said.

"Never mind," the policeman snapped. "Go and fetch your clothes."

They were going through my bedroom cupboards now, scattering clothes all over the floor as I dressed. Stompie Lategan stood at the door. As I stooped to fasten my shoes, he bent to retrieve a discarded envelope from the carpet.

"Trust me." It was less than a whisper.

Fiona rushed into the room. "The telephone is out of order," she screamed. "I'm going mad! Do you hear me, mad!"

"Mrs. Pendrake." Stompie's tone was cold. "Your telephone has been disconnected. It will be reconnected at the discretion of the authorities. Meanwhile, if you are not

161

familiar with the law, madam, any comment on this night, or for that matter, any complaint or enquiry may well place you beyond the law. I advise you to retire to bed, madam."

Fiona looked from Stompie to me. "Oh," she said. "Oh, of course." She returned to her bedroom.

As we marched down the passage, three policemen came out of my study carrying bulging canvas bags containing my papers. A policeman unhooked the handcuffs from his belt. "That will not be necessary," said Stompie. "The detainee will drive with me. I want one car ahead, and one covering the rear."

I followed Stompie out of the house. We all piled into the vehicles.

"Stompie, what in God's name is happening?" I asked as we drove off.

He leaned down and unplugged an intercom on the dashboard. "They arrested Kobie," he said hoarsely. "He gave your name. When we get there, say nothing and do nothing. Now be quiet."

He reconnected the intercom. "One, two, Z zero calling." He spoke into the microphone. "One hundred twenty kilometers, destination Roeland Street."

We drove fast through the sleeping city. The prison gates swung wide as our headlights hit the great studded portal. The cars drew up in the courtyard of the jail. A guard ran up to open the car door for Stompie. The man saluted and stood stiffly to attention.

"Take over, Sergeant." Stompie marched off into the night.

How does one describe the peculiar cowing of the spirit which sudden arrest by ruthless authority in the middle of the night can wreak? They marched me into an office. Six burly guards stood grimly in the light of a naked bulb. A pair of heavy boots rested on a neat pile of dun-colored clothes. "Change into these garments," a guard commanded.

162

They watched me as I changed. "Your underclothes too," the guard said. Out of habit I began folding my trousers. "Never mind that. Drop them."

The man behind the desk nodded to one of his colleagues. "Follow that man," he told me. I left my clothes in a heap on the floor. They led me to another wing of the building where I was locked into a cell with one tiny window near the ceiling.

The sun was high when they came back and opened the cell door. Once again I was brought into the office, where they took my fingerprints.

"You have been granted house arrest," a guard said.

He proceeded to read the conditions governing house arrest. "At any time of the day or night, an officer or officers will be entitled to enter your place of residence to ensure strict observation of the aforementioned conditions pertaining to house arrest. If at any time the conditions and regulations are contravened, you will immediately be imprisoned at the discretion of the investigating officer."

He tapped his desk with a pencil. My passport, I saw, lay on the blotter. "Your passport has been confiscated. If at any time you should desire to leave the country, you have the right to apply for an exit visa at the discretion of the appropriate minister." He smiled sourly. "Your clothes have been deposited in your cell. In fifteen minutes, transport will be provided to convey you to your place of residence."

Fiona was out when I got home. I wandered through the house, trying to collect my scattered thoughts. The terms and conditions of my house arrest thrummed through my head.

I was sitting in my study when Stompie Lategan arrived, accompanied by a plainclothesman. He saluted me formally at the front door. "Wait in the car," he told the plainclothesman.

He looked at me directly for a moment. Then he took off his cap and walked ahead of me towards my study. His eyes swept round the cornice of the ceiling. He moved around the room, running a hand behind each picture. He peered into the fireplace. He shifted the carpet on the stone floor with his foot. Then he closed the door and sat down in an easy chair.

"Stompie," I said, "for God's sake, what is this all about?"

He looked at me levelly. "Kobie September was taken the day before yesterday. I told you he gave your name. He was injured — very badly injured. They amputated his leg this morning." Stompie pointed to the middle of his left thigh.

"Dear God," I said. "What has he done? Why was I arrested?"

Stompie dropped his eyes. "Investigations are proceeding."

"And Carla — what about his wife Carla?"

"She is under house arrest."

"Why? Christ, why?"

"Time will tell." Stompie rose to his feet.

"And Gammatjie and Fatima?"

"They are being detained. Take care, Paul. This is serious."

He moved into the passage and out into the hall. "Your telephone has been reconnected," he said. "Use it with utmost discretion." He took his cap from the hall table. The plainclothesman was standing at the door.

"You have been warned," Stompie said loudly. "We shall be back." Again he saluted formally.

I picked up the telephone. It had been reconnected. I dialed the office and the secretary answered.

"Miss Perks, please tell Dr. Bentwhistle that I have the flu. I shall have to go to bed. Please cancel all my appointments."

"Oh, I am sorry, doctor," she said sympathetically. "Now don't you worry. I'll take care of everything."

"Please telephone the medical director of the hospital and tell him, would you?"

164

"Shall I ask Dr. Bentwhistle to call on you?"

"No, Miss Perks, I shall telephone if I need anything, thank you." I hung up.

Fiona came home for lunch. "What a mess you have made of things," she spat at me.

I began to explain the circumstances, but it only made her angrier.

"I warned you about those wretched coloreds! Why in heaven's name if you had to prowl about, could you not have shown a shade of discretion, not to mention self-respect? What am I going to tell people?" She flung her handbag across the hall table. "So you are under house arrest. Do you know what that means? No more than two people at any time. Well, you'll have to eat in your study. I'm not going to live like an outcast. An outcast, that is what you are, an outcast!"

"I must tell you that the telephone is tapped," I said.

"Oh my God! And where is my passport?"

"It was in my desk with my other papers." I confess I smiled then.

"Damn you," Fiona said. "Damn you!"

I shall never know whether it was Dr. le Bois or Fiona or neither who leaked the news, but somebody did. On the third morning I received two letters. One was from Reggie Bentwhistle, regretting recent events but confident that I would fully appreciate just how incompatible current circumstance was to the conduct of our type of practice. In terms of our contract he would be happy to accept my resignation.

The other was from Dr. Krag, medical director of the hospital. Dr. Krag wished to draw my attention to Section 207, subsection (f) of the Provincial Ordinance 1961, which forbade any person employed in provincial government service from being actively involved in politics. He expressed appreciation of long years of honorary service in the hospital.

I was totally alone.

House arrest. What a benign-sounding phrase!

Does empathy ever extend beyond the range of personal experience?

For how many years had I been fully aware of the fact that many of my fellow countrymen — black, colored, and white — were under house arrest, and others detained in jail indefinitely for obscure political transgressions. But, I had reasoned, the law is the law, and until such time as it is changed, it must be observed. There was always the vague hope that someday, somehow, things would improve. And the comforting feeling that none of this was my doing. The government was responsible. Besides, things were so much worse in other parts of the world. So what could an apolitical individual like myself actually do except get on with his job, and generally make the best of things?

How can I convey the spiritual death of house arrest? The deprivation of the privilege and the therapy of work; the indignity of twice daily reporting to a police station where frequent changes of uniformed youths searched through an ever-expanding file to correlate my face with their photograph; the anxious care to avoid the company of more than two people at any time; the dread of embarrassing or implicating family or friends. The constant impotent anxiety about Kobie and Carla; the callous indifference of my son Jeremy; the humiliation of encountering acquaintances on the street or in a store, and seeing them turn away hurriedly; the peal of the doorbell in the small hours of the night; the mysterious telephone calls which clicked dead as I answered; the disappearance of colored servants fearing for their safety. The total uncertainty as to the past, present, or future.

How could anyone, except a fellow detainee, really understand the spiritual fragmentation of those anxious months?

I was in the shower when the bell rang. I dried hurriedly, grabbed a robe, and ran to the door.

Stompie Lategan stood on the porch. He was unshaven; his uniform was crumpled. The bright morning sun accentuated deep shadows in a haggard face. His shoulders slumped. There was death in his eyes.

We stood like that for a long moment. "Stompie," I said, "are you hurt?"

"Paul!" He rubbed a hand across his forehead. "Paul!"

I took his arm and led him to my study. He collapsed into a chair, burying his face in his hands.

"I could not stop that bastard Kruger," he groaned. "Paul, can you understand, I could not stop him." His eyes were pleading.

"What are trying to tell me, Stompie?"

He told me Kobie's story then. Not the whole of it; but my lifelong knowledge of Kobie, familiarity with place and circumstance, and the unrelenting gnaw of conscience have conspired to paint a picture which will haunt me for the rest of my life.

23

That section of the False Bay coast is familiar to me — an unbroken arc of twenty or more miles of empty beach stretching from Muizenberg to Gordon's Bay. It forms the southern rim of the sandy waste linking the Cape Peninsula to the mainland.

At low tide on fine summer mornings, the firm sand shines like glass in the sun. To the west the naval station at Simonstown shimmers like a mirage above the sea, and far to the east the blue peaks of the Langeberg Mountains, scored by the long man-made sweep of Sir Lowry's Pass, frame the bay.

On such days, periwinkles, mussels, and all manner of tidal creatures take advantage of the brief exposure of their domain, leaving tracks in the smooth wet sand as they converge to feed on stranded jellyfish. Gulls wheel overhead, and red-legged oyster catchers skitter along the sand to fly shrilly across the water at your approach. Sometimes porpoises frolic in the gentle surf.

Occasionally, prompted by uncanny instinct, colored fishermen come down from the dunes to launch a boat and draw a net around a passing school of harder or mackerel. Then, as the glistening silver and blue harvest flip-flops on the sand, there is laughter and shouting on the beach. The air is clear and heavy with ozone. The sun is warm on the skin. The material pursuits of mankind seem ridiculously remote, and one feels that God is in His heaven.

But when the boisterous southeaster or the northwest gales of winter lash False Bay into a frenzy, the great rollers of the Indian Ocean assault the shore as if determined to regain their lost ground. Then the winds streak across the beach, blasting the sand into blinding, skin-flaying drifts; and wisps of blown sand trail like smoke from the crests of the desolate ever-changing dunes.

When Kobie left District VI on that fateful night, he drove straight to the house of the Imam on the Cape Flats. I had met the Imam once in Gammatjie's house. He was a slightly built man in his middle fifties. Steel-rimmed spectacles accentuated the scholarly character of a finely molded face.

The Imam, Kobie found, was strangely reluctant to help.

"Are you from the police, Mr. September?" the Imam asked.

"No," Kobie said. "No, I am not. But . . ."

The Imam smiled blandly. "What then is your interest in this matter, Mr. September? Perhaps it is best forgotten. These are difficult times, Mr. September. Perhaps we should leave these matters to the authorities."

Kobie controlled his impatience. "My interest lies in the fact that I must protect my family. Achmat Salie said that you might be able to help."

The Imam dropped his gaze. "Achmat Salie has always spoken very highly of you, Mr. September . . . It is rumored that there is a place in the dunes where a man called George Paku gives young men instruction . . ." He shrugged. "It may be no more than idle gossip."

"Which dunes?"

"Perhaps the dunes beyond Muizenberg may be a likely place. People live there. It would seem to be a good place to start if you were so minded. I have not seen you this night," the Imam said as he closed the door.

Kobie drove back along the National Road. Instead of continuing into the city, he skirted Rondebosch Common and drove past Kenilworth Race Course to reach Prince George's Drive. He pushed the big Dodge on past Zeekoe Vlei. There he saw the first of them — a cluster of tumble-down shacks fashioned out of rusty corrugated iron, planks, and other remnants of demolition.

I knew of these squatters — colored vagrants who flocked into Cape Town in search of work which they hoped the official banishment of black labor would soon make available. Destitute and without shelter, they rigged their primitive hovels in an area where no man would voluntarily live, and which, it was rumored, the authorities might in the future proclaim a Colored Group Area.

Vainly Kobie searched for an access road. Finally he parked his car in a thicket of willow and proceeded on foot. The settlement was far more extensive than he had anticipated. Thousands of shacks crouched at random among the dunes. Mangy dogs growled and snarled whenever his progress took him too near the undefined territory of a dwelling. The willows whipped back and forth in gusts of wind. A pale moon rose in the east.

Kobie knew the suspicion which such people harbored against any intrusion by strangers. He pressed on in the hope of finding some clue, or some acquaintance he might question.

The houses were more scattered now. Ahead he heard the roar of the surf. Soon he approached the long ribbon of the Strandfontein Road. He crossed the road and climbed a dune to scan the area.

Almost at his feet a pair of legs protruded from under a bush. The body lay on its stomach, sheltered from the wind in the lee of the dune. Below the hiss of the wind, heavy snores grated in the bush. Watching the legs, Kobie lit a cigarette. The man did not stir. Kobie moved closer and held the burning cigarette under the man's nose.

170

"Huh?" The sleeper opened heavy eyes. There was a waft of stale wine as he coughed and spat into the sand. He sat up. With trembling fingers he accepted the cigarette.

Kobie allowed several minutes to pass. His companion was obviously not suspicious or aggressive. The drunk drew deeply on his cigarette, inhaling the smoke to the bottom of his lungs, rinsing it round his mouth with hollowed brown cheeks.

"Ever heard of a man called George?" Kobie asked.

"Silly bugger," the drunk said. "Dangerous, mind you. Him and his church and his skollies with dogs."

"He is a good man," Kobie murmured. "You should listen to George."

"You can listen," the man said. "For myself I want a quiet life. With people like George, you can easily land in jail. I've just got out."

"How do I reach George's place from this side?"

The man lifted his body on one elbow and pointed along the beach. "Ag, man, it's just round the corner. There beyond the place where the army had its cannons in the war. You know the old army huts. That is where George holds his church."

Kobie rose to his feet. "What time is George's church?" He took a handful of cigarettes from his pocket and handed them to the man.

"When it's dark." The man yawned loudly and rolled on-to his face.

The night wind was cold. Kobie found the hut and lay flat on the sand among some bushes, watching. Over a period of an hour, he counted fourteen men entering the hut, some alone, some in pairs. Among them came Red Fink with his dog. When the moon set, Kobie crept closer. He made for the far end of the building opposite the door. He detected a murmur of voices inside the building. A chink of light penciled through a crack in the boarded wall. He crept closer and listened.

171

". . . Here a man is not a man," the voice was saying. Kobie recognized the accent, well disguised as it was. If this was George Paku's voice, George was a black.

". . . He is a member of some group and his life must conform to the white man's rule," the voice continued. "The disease feeds on itself. Now the white government's nightmare is that its apartheid creations will fall into anti-apartheid hands. A minority cannot indefinitely keep a majority down. The whites in this country have placed themselves on a path of no return. Are the whites committed to a policy of nonviolence? Why then should the colored man be committed to nonviolence? The colored man would be a fool if he tried to follow the path of nonviolence. This land belongs to us all. We must fight."

Listening outside the wall, Kobie heard a murmur of assent from other voices within the hut.

"Now for our instructions . . ." the voice continued. "Last time we demonstrated the petrol bomb and the bucket bomb for distribution of propaganda leaflets. Are there any questions?"

Kobie loosened his knife from its sheath. The speaker, he now knew, must be a communist operator. Red Fink was here as a guard. He must lure Red Fink away. His quarrel was with Red Fink.

Kobie searched among the undergrowth and found a stone. Then, moving around the building, he threw it with all his might at the door of the hut. At once the door flew wide and Red Fink and his dog stood silhouetted against the light. Kobie shook the bushes in front of him. The dog growled and strained forward. Now more figures pressed round the door. Nose to the ground, the dog came across the sand. Kobie rushed forward. The dog hurled itself at his throat. Diverting the brute's attack with a sweep of his left arm, Kobie drove the knife into the dog's ribs. He felt the hot flush of blood over his hand. Red Fink came at him, crouching low. Encumbered by the body of the big dog, Kobie turned too late. Red Fink's knife sank into his groin.

172

Kobie's massive fist gripped Red Fink's hair and pulled the head back. Red Fink screamed. Kobie drew the edge of his knife across the extended throat. The scream ended in a gurgle.

He saw them running now, figure after figure silhouetted briefly in the oblong light at the door of the hut, fleeing like rats flushed from a barn. A wave of giddiness blurred Kobie's vision. He shook his head. His trousers were soaked with blood. He tested the leg. He could bend it but he could not straighten the knee. The leg buckled under him as he tried to stand. He rolled in the sand. He must find something to stanch the wound. On hands and knees, he crept across the sand. Keeping to the shadows, he hoisted himself erect by the doorpost and looked into the hut. Except for one man bending over an assortment of equipment, the brightly lit room was empty. The man was uncoiling a roll of something which looked like electric wiring. Kobie saw the man take out a box of matches and walk towards a blanket-draped window. Clarity rushed through Kobie's mind. The man was lighting a fuse. Kobie yelled.

The man turned. At the door stood a giant. A bigger man than he had ever seen. In one bloodstained hand, a dripping knife was poised aloft. The face looked ashen.

The man lit the fuse and, kicking out the frame of the window, escaped into the night.

At the door, Kobie fought to retain consciousness. He saw the bright star running along the fuse wire. Summoning his last reserve of strength he dragged himself forward across the floor. Less than a foot from the stacked gelignite, he crushed the fuse wire in his fist.

At five o'clock in the morning an office cleaner from the settlement, hurrying across the dunes to catch a lift on the Strandfontein Road, found the bodies of Red Fink and his dog. She reported it to the police.

"That is how it all started," Stompie said. "That bloody George Paku was a communist agent. We threw the biggest

173

net on record round the country. Everyone remotely associated, including you, Paul, was pulled in. In two days we had more than a hundred people behind bars. Then George Paku squealed. He told us everything, even before Kruger got at him."

"What about Kobie? What about Kobie?" I pressed him.

For a second, Stompie's eyes blazed with almost maniacal rage. He leapt from his chair and paced across the room. When he turned his face had crumpled again. "For Christ's sake, let me talk Paul. Can't you see that I must talk . . . For God's sake, let me talk."

How often had I witnessed this syndrome in my consulting room. People, usually strong decent people buffeted by fate, confused by circumstance, or hounded by conscience to a point where the only tenuous link with sanity is dependent on the opportunity to talk.

I poured Stompie another brandy.

"Is there never any middle road, Paul?" He gave a deep sigh. "Is there ever anything more than compromise? I told you George squealed, but you know, Paul, it was not because he was frightened . . . He was tired, Paul, and sick at heart."

Then Stompie told me George Paku's story.

24

"It all started more than ten years ago," Stompie said. "At the time of the banning of the African National Congress — you remember, Paul?"

"Vaguely."

"Well, this George Paku was born on the farm Neville's Rest in the Eastern Province. Because George showed remarkable intelligence, the owner of the farm, Tom Quentin, sent him to the Catholic Mission School in nearby Queenstown. When he matriculated, he chose to become a teacher at the Mission School.

"He joined the African National Congress, and was a member of the A.N.C. delegation which approached the prime minister for reconsideration of the Pass Laws, the Group Areas Act, and the Suppression of Communism Act. The government's response was a warning against any contravention of the law of the land. Then the black people lost faith in their A.N.C. leaders. They rioted. The government reacted with even more drastic measures — the Public Safety Act and the Criminal Law Amendment Act — which might interpret anything, even assistance given to families of detainees, as subversion.

"When the police came for George Paku, he could name no place as home. His house was the Mission School. But he

175

wasn't allowed to stay there, so he gave the name of the farm where he was born. Tom Quentin agreed to give George Paku shelter. He also undertook to report any transgression of the banning order to the police.

"I flew up there myself to see Tom Quentin," Stompie said. "A first class man. The Quentins are 1820 settler stock. The family have owned Neville's Rest for over a century. Tom Quentin corroborated every word of George Paku's story.

"It was the year when the wool boom was at its peak. Skilled African labor, lured away by contract work in the mines, was scarce. The sheep had to be shorn, so Quentin hired the itinerant services of the Acme Machine Shearing Company of Australasia. A man called Cobber Horbek was the foreman.

"Interpol found Horbek for us in Sydney. We sent a man to Australia to interview him. A miserable bastard, raised in an orphanage, served a term in jail for robbery with violence . . . it was as a prisoner of war in Korea that Horbek became a communist agent. Unfortunately we had nothing on him really. We could not get an extradition order.

"Anyway, George Paku was the best shearer Tom Quentin had working for him. Horbek noticed George working alone in a corner of the shearing shed, and asked Quentin about him. Quentin explained that George was under a banning order for five years.

"That night Horbek visited George in his hut, and convinced him that he couldn't help his people while he was stuck on Quentin's farm, that he should leave the country.

"Four nights later George Paku made his way to a deserted stretch of the Transkei Coast, where he was picked up by a rubber dinghy and taken out to a Russian submarine.

"You should have heard the poor devil describing the communist training camp in Odessa," Stompie said. "He told us about one time when all thirty-five trainees were

176

made to stand in a circle with fixed bayonets. Then they led in a young Arab, a boy of no more than eighteen or nineteen; George never knew his name or what he was supposed to have done. He was barefooted, with a chain between his ankles. His hands were stiff and bleeding where his fingernails had been torn out; his face was bruised and his hair matted with blood. He had confessed to the failure of his mission, they said. The enemy had gained information from his defection. When the guard removed the cloth from his eyes, the Arab boy stood blinded by the sun. Then he screamed, seeing where he was. The guard uncoiled his whip and the steel-tipped lash bit into the boy's back. He tried to run in his chains, a shambling gait like a baboon, using his arms to assist his shackled legs. Everywhere the boy ran the bayonets gleamed and each time he turned from their menace, the long whip lashed out. Finally he threw himself onto a bayonet, and the huge Nigerian holding the gun lifted the body and threw it into the dust, as one would a bundle of hay.

"In that camp George learned it all — the fundamentals of Marxism, the psychology of terrorism, sabotage, subversion, and propaganda. Above all he learned that he, George Paku, was irrevocably committed and entirely disposable. Then there followed the long trek through Tanzania, the raids into what was to become Zambia, the raids into Mozambique, and finally into southern Rhodesia . . . shooting, running, and killing. Then back to Moscow for a refresher course. He had been selected for a special mission.

"The poor bastard had come to realize that the communists were only using the distress of his people to further their own ends. But whenever the thought of escape entered his mind, he remembered the Arab boy in the training camp in Odessa.

"George Paku's special mission was Cape Town, where he was to channel the discontent among the Cape Colored people into open revolt. He was smuggled into Cape Town in the hold of a ship, dressed as a dockworker.

"When we caught up with him, Paku could not recall how long it had been since that night he had fled from the hut on the dunes," Stompie said. "When the charge didn't explode he was afraid to go back to the hut. So he made his way to a store which was his contact with the regional command, but they were waiting for him with a gun. Evidently one of his trainees had been a spy and the failure of his mission had been reported. His long years of terrorist training stood him in good stead, though, and he managed to get away. He stole some mechanic's overalls from a filling station and tore up his own clothes. In this disguise he started walking.

"He must have walked over six hundred miles before we caught up with him. He walked at night and lay low in the day. At one point, driven by hunger, he got a job as a sewage-removal hand in a village — a job nobody wanted. Despite his care, one of his colored co-workers spotted an inflection in his speech and accused him of being a Kaffir, so he moved on.

"Finally, a white woman caught him stealing food from a pile of supplies behind a house — he was close to starvation by then — and she telephoned the police. They found him walking on the road to Queenstown.

"He just told us the whole bloody story. He did not give a damn. He was tired, Paul — tired of living. He had believed — yes, believed as I once believed, Paul."

"What will happen to him now?"

"They'll hang him," Stompie said.

"And Kobie? What about Kobie?"

Stompie covered his face with his hands. "Oh God!"

I took him by the shoulders and shook him. "Tell me!"

"Paul, I could not control Kruger," he groaned. "I could not control him. He is a BOSS man. BOSS is like the Gestapo, Paul. They are not concerned with state security . . . their concern is the security of the Broederbond. BOSS, believe me, is above the law. Kruger never stops. He is an animal. God, he never stops."

"Stops what?"

Stompie took a long labored breath. His eyes were haunted.

"I was there," he said. "I did not want to be there but I felt it was the least I could do. I could not stay away. Kruger had Kobie strapped to the chair. They had a buzzer strapped over his ears, and the electric crawler implanted in his scrotum. God, Paul, he was no longer a man. Once or twice I thought he recognized me, but he gave no sign.

"Kruger kept saying the same things over and over. 'You would like to help us wouldn't you? You would like your wife and child to be safe, wouldn't you? It could happen to anyone, couldn't it? These communists are cunning. They promise the earth, don't they? You were only trying to do what you thought was right, weren't you? You meant no harm. We all understand that. Now what were the names of your associates? If you tell me, you will be well cared for. Your wife and son will be well cared for. You served your country with honor during the war. Now serve your country again.'

"God, Paul, Kruger kept on and on . . . and do you know, Paul, smashed as he was, Kobie was his own man. He did not give an inch. I think that's what riled Kruger's guts. He could not touch him. Kobie must have been as strong as a lion."

"What do you mean, 'must have been'?"

Stompie did not seem to hear me. "Kobie appeared to be unconscious. There was no response when Kruger's men threw the electric switch. I could see that Kruger was tired. They'd been at it all night. 'Give him some air,' he said. 'Open the window and remove the straps.' He said he planned to resume the workout in one hour. They left me alone with Kobie."

"Stompie, for God's sake . . ."

"Paul," Stompie asked softly, "have you ever seen a man's eyes talk to you?"

"Yes," I said, "I have."

179

"Well then you will understand . . . Paul, Kobie had known I was there all the time. I helped him to stand. He leaned on my shoulder. With three agonizing hops he got to the window. Then he shook me off. He stood straight as an arrow. Paul, the dawn was just breaking. We could smell the sea. Then he said, 'Baas Stompie, look after Carla and my son . . . also Baas Paul' . . . Then he jumped . . ."

"Oh, Christ!"

"Paul, he could not have lived like that . . . Besides, Kruger could not afford to let him live."

We sat quietly for long minutes, Stompie and I. Then I said, "Kobie would, I think, have done the same for you."

"I think so . . . I pray so."

"And what about Carla?"

"She will be given an exit visa," Stompie said. "She will leave for Rome shortly."

"I must see her."

"Of course . . . of course . . ."

"Have you forgotten that I am under house arrest?"

"Your order has been rescinded," Stompie said. "They have always known that you were clean. You are well known. Having pulled you in, the BOSS people had to justify the arrest, and keep you quiet. They think that way . . . Believe me, they are as scared as hell."

"My God . . ." My mind spun. "My God . . . But I have no official notification of my release."

"You will get it." Stompie stood up gravely. "God help us. I'm going to see Carla now . . . Believe me, I'll do anything in my power to help you both. I'll keep in touch."

It was on the first page of the evening paper: "DETAINEE JACOBUS SEPTEMBER FALLS FROM TENTH-FLOOR WINDOW."

A spokesman for the Ministry of Justice stated that the detainee was believed to have been delirious as the result of a prolonged hunger strike.

25

The man from BOSS returned from the telephone. He spoke quietly to his colleague. Together they approached the woman with the fur coat.

"We must search your hand luggage, madam."

She was indignant. "It has already been done on the docks. I paid what they asked."

"This is a routine security measure, madam."

In the process of rearranging her numerous parcels she dropped her handbag. Lipstick, compact, and an assortment of contents rolled across the floor. I helped her husband retrieve the bits.

The BOSS men apparently found nothing of interest. They moved towards the other two passengers.

"Thank you, sir. Thank you so much." The woman smiled at me. She drew out a chair at the bare table. "Won't you join us?" She held out a hand. "I am Mrs. Polak . . . Mrs. Rachel Polak. This is my husband, Mr. Isidore Polak."

"Pendrake," I said, "Paul Pendrake."

She was pouring me coffee. "Are you flying to Johannesburg?"

"No," I said. "No, I am not."

"And what business are you in?"

"None, really," I said. "I'm a doctor."

"A doctor, eh? A doctor, uh-huh? Our son Max is a doctor. We have just visited him in Israel. He works in a tent, on a kibbutz. In a tent, will you believe it, doctor? He treats everybody — even Arabs — for nothing, for nothing. My brother, Gerald Shait, is also a doctor, in Johannesburg. You must know him, doctor. He begged my son Max to come into partnership. My brother is making a fortune . . . a fortune." Mrs. Polak shrugged. "I don't know what's the matter with the young people these days."

"Neither do I," I said.

"My son Max wants us to come and live in Israel; but doctor, my husband and I were born in Johannesburg. All right, we have the blacks here — in Israel they have the Arabs, so what is the difference?"

She rummaged in her bag and pulled out her business card, handing it to me. I read: "Très Sportif — 2009 Ebden Street, Johannesburg." She was peering at me expectantly.

"That's French, you know, doctor. If ever you and your wife come to Johannesburg, look us up. No obligation. It will be a pleasure to see you."

She lifted a corner of the plastic cover to reveal the hem of the fur coat. "This is our newest line — made of genuine goatskin and fully lined throughout with an applique of Siberian wolf. Who could tell the difference, doctor, and half the price retail. We cater to the smart woman, you see doctor . . . I'm sure your wife is very smart."

I slipped the card in my pocket. "Thank you," I said.

The young man from BOSS came across the restaurant. "Come," he said. "My orders are that all passengers must be concentrated in the restaurant lobby."

The crowd outside was still slow-clapping. Thrump . . . thrump . . . thrump . . . thrump . . . the measured beat pulsed through the building with unnerving persistence.

Just then Stompie Lategan strode into the restaurant. He came straight across to me. I rose and moved forward to meet him. His eyes, it seemed, were everywhere, probing

182

and watchful. For a second I had a vision of a young Stompie Lategan in blue and white striped rugby jersey marshaling his team. He reached into a pocket of his tunic and drew out an envelope.

"Paul," he said softly, "this is serious. We've been informed that there is a bomb in this terminal. We are safe as long as we hold Carla, but when the plane is clear . . . The thing must be somewhere. They" — he indicated the crowd outside with a jerk of his head — "are only waiting for Carla to leave, but they are getting out of control. We cannot hold the plane any longer. We must get her out . . ."

"But Stompie . . ."

He turned in the direction of the waiting aircraft. I saw Carla and Roberto, escorted by two men with automatic rifles, walking across the apron towards the big jet.

"Here." Stompie handed me the envelope. "Your official release from house arrest . . . and take this . . ." He passed me a key. "If things break, go through the restaurant kitchen. There is a door in the far corner. It leads into the V.I.P. lounge. The fire escape opens out at the end of the building. A car is parked there . . . a cream-colored Ford. This is the key."

"But I have my own car."

"This crowd will never let you reach your car. Drive out onto the airfield and right along the strip. All air traffic has been suspended. There is a gate at the far end." He pointed north.

The other passengers were clustering around now.

"Officer, officer," Mrs. Polak pleaded. "Officer, you must help us. What is happening? I have not seen my children for two months. We paid our fare in advance . . . I've told my husband we must sue . . ."

"I'm sorry, madam," Stompie said. "Please be calm. We're doing our best." He turned to the men from BOSS. "Dr. Pendrake is no longer under surveillance . . . Escort these passengers to the aircraft."

"*Ja*, Colonel."

I watched Carla climb the stairs into the aircraft. She hesitated briefly and waved in the direction of the terminal. Automatically I waved back. Then she ducked into the plane.

The passengers were collecting their hand luggage.

"Paul, come with me," Stompie said.

In the restaurant kitchen he unlocked a door marked "Staff Only." I followed him up a narrow steel stair leading to a catwalk high over the main concourse. Through the high windows I could see the crowd, at least five thousand people. Menace emanated from the slow-clapping mass like heat above coals. The thin line of the riot squad and their dogs looked desperately inadequate.

"Eeeeeeeh. Yah . . . Eeeeeeeh. Yah . . . Eeeeeeeh. Yah . . ." Deep in the body of the crowd the high-pitched scream of a black woman rose. The wail seemed to fill the sky. The slow-clapping stopped. The crowd stood silent. "Eeeeeeeh . . ." It was a savage primitive exhortation from the beginning of time.

Inside the concourse, led by the man from BOSS, the passengers trailed wearily across the hall. Stompie gripped my arm and pointed.

Outside a young man broke from the crowd, a tall slender figure with a white skullcap on the back of his head. His long robe fluttered as he ran. He clutched what looked like a a briefcase to his chest. A police dog bounded at him, shredding his robe. He shook the dog off, leaving it worrying at a long tatter of cloth. Still he came on. A shot rang out. The young man balked. As I watched, a red stain spread across his belly. Then he came on, lurching and weaving. There was a rattle of automatic fire. He fell to his knees, shook his head, rose shakily and staggered on. The riod squad converged. He was out of sight now, somewhere below us, near the wall.

"This is it," I heard Stompie say. He dragged out his intercom. "Get that plane in the air. Get that plane off the ground! Take off! Take off! Take off!" Then he leaned over the inner railing, cupping his hands over his mouth. "Move!" he yelled. "Move!" His voice echoed through the hall. "Move on! Move on!"

I saw one of the men from BOSS turn a sunglassed face upwards.

I do not recall hearing the bomb explode. Suddenly below me the small file of passengers, the men from BOSS, and all the furniture moved like leaves swept by a giant broom. The woman with the fur coat cartwheeled through the air. Shots . . . shouts . . . and a roar. Below us the crowd poured through the hole in the wall. Stompie was on his knees by the railing.

They came like ants, trampling over each other, driven by a blind release of hate. A large black led the throng, smashing the scattered seats, kicking at the strewn corpses of the passengers. I watched the big black pick up the fur coat, tie the sleeves round his neck and caper about. Stompie was on his feet now, firing his automatic into the milling crowd below.

"Go, Paul! Go!" he commanded.

A pickax head, hurled from below, struck Stompie on his shoulder. It bounced off to crash through the glass expanse of window behind us. He crumpled for a moment.

"What about you?" I asked.

He turned and shoved his gun into my ribs. "Go!" he shouted. "For Christ's sake, go or I'll blow you to hell!"

I ran along the catwalk towards the restaurant kitchen. Below in the concourse the crowd, momentarily diverted by Stompie's firing, seethed and bellowed in frustration. A hail of missiles came up at me. Above the turmoil I heard the full-throttled whine of the Boeing's jets as the plane tore down the runway for takeoff.

The kitchen was deserted. So was the V.I.P. lounge. They came swarming round the runway just as I started the Ford. Bottles and stones clattered over the car, smashing the rear window. I accelerated. A man with outstretched arms tried to block my way. I ran him down. The car lurched over the body. The runway opened ahead. I shoved my foot flat down.

The gate at the end of the runway was closed. I drew up. It was unlocked. High in the western sky I caught the glint of sun on silver fuselage. The aircraft banked in a wide arc, then leveled out on course. I watched the ever-diminishing speck disappear in the haze above the mountains to the north.

A blinding flash split the sky above the distant terminal. An instant later the shock wave sent me sprawling in the sand. I drew myself to my knees. Against the western sky a giant mushroom of destruction billowed and rolled above the inferno of the fuel storage depot.

The red ball of the sun glowed lurid through the spreading pall of black smoke. The hot breath of the inferno drifted on the thin wind. Short sharp detonations punctuated the blast. I recognized grenades and anti-personnel shells. The reinforcements were moving in. Above me I heard the staccato whir of a helicopter. I stood up and waved. A stream of tracer bullets stitched a row between me and the Ford. I dove into the bushes for cover. The chopper circled low, then slanted off towards the blazing terminal.

As I knelt there in the sand beneath the empty sky, I was alone as I had never before been alone . . . alone and terrified.

26

At last I got to my feet and ran for the Ford. The engine started at once, and I drove fast through the gate. At the main highway I turned away from the city.

To the north the blue peaks of the Drakenstein Mountains were etched against the sky. I pushed the accelerator hard to the floor.

Faster I raced, skirting the ancient town of Stellenbosch and on into the tortuous bends of the Helshoogte Pass. Through great defiles shrouded in the black shadows of towering buttresses of blue granite. Through sun-kissed vales where stately Cape Dutch farmsteads nestled among their vineyards. Colored farm children waved from the roadside. White geese grazed around a sudden pond. Deeper and deeper I raced into the peace of the mountains, then down the long leafy descent. The Franschhoek Valley lay before me.

I was sweating. My breath came in great gulps. I turned the Ford off the road and parked in a clearing under spreading oaks. A hundred yards to the right a laborer's cottage smiled in a poplar grove. Blue smoke curled from the chimney. Hens scratched busily among the leaves. A young colored woman with a toddler clutching her skirt came from the house.

I found that it hurt my neck to turn my head, but I followed them with my eyes until they passed from sight, then reappeared in the rearview mirror. The woman took a hatchet from her girdle, wrenched branches from a pile of brush and hacked kindling. The ax blows echoed through the stillness.

The toddler wandered out of view. My head throbbed. Then there was a rustling in the scrub beside the car, and the child stood there curious-eyed, naked except for a ragged cotton vest stretched over a shiny brown belly. As I moved to face the child his lower lip trembled into a pout and his face crumpled. Then he screamed, a long, high-pitched yell of terror. In the rearview mirror I saw the woman turn and run toward the car. She swept the child into her arms and turned fiercely on me. Then I saw her eyes soften.

"Baas Paul," she whispered. She dropped the hatchet and set the child down. "Baas Paul, you're hurt." Her face was full of concern.

I touched the right side of my face, and the hand I withdrew was bloody.

"Baas Paul, don't you remember me? This is Sarie — Sarie Witbooi. I'm Andries' daughter, Andries from Fleur. What has happened to you? I must call Baas Pieter Ferriera."

I knew who she was then. Andries Witbooi had always lived at Fleur. He was Uncle Gert's right-hand man.

"No," I said, "don't call anyone." I was not sure where Pieter Ferriera stood.

She looked at me intently, brow furrowed, eyes knowing. "You are in trouble, Baas Paul?"

"Yes — yes, I think I have been."

She opened the car door and helped me toward the cottage. "Please let me call Baas Pieter Ferriera."

My legs moved automatically. The warm smell of her bare neck under my arm was comforting. "No, Sarie, better not."

188

"Come, Baas Paul. Only a little further."

The interior of the cottage was dim and cool and sparsely furnished with a deal table and four chairs. On a pine dresser, neat rows of unmatched cups and saucers glistened on shelves decorated with fringes of intricately cut newspaper. A wedding photograph of Sarie and her husband in ill-fitting black church suit hung on the wall. A fire glowed in a massive iron stove. The room smelt of food, warmth, and humanity. The far end of the room was curtained off for sleeping quarters.

Sarie sat me down at the table. I felt her hands part my hair.

"Baas Paul, I must wash your face. First I must boil some water, then put on some iodine. You see, I took a Red Cross course once . . ." She smiled shyly at me. "Ag, here I am telling a doctor what to do."

I watched her take a blue roll of cotton wool from a drawer in the dresser. "Once, Baas Paul, when my man Hendrick Filander put a pitchfork through his foot, I followed the instructions and the wound healed in no time. He was back at work in two days."

The child wrapped himself around the door post and sucked his thumb. Sarie was at the stove. "Ag, how I wish my man Filander was here. Why should he take the truck to the Co-op just when I need him?" She was talking to herself.

I felt her hands on my head again. Gently she washed my face. Blood-stained cotton wool swabs dropped into a basin with a wet plop.

"This is going to hurt, Baas Paul." The sting of the iodine on my forehead seared through my body. "There, there, it is all clean — the cut is deep but the bleeding has stopped. Soon it will be all better; there will not even be a mark." She was drying my face. "Now let me get you some coffee, Baas Paul. The nurse at the Red Cross said coffee with sugar is very good — for shock, you know."

"Ag, Baas Paul, is it not terrible about Kobie September? Some people say he was right to go after that Kaffir who threatened his wife, but Baas Pieter Ferriera says he must have been mixed up in some dirty business or he would have left the matter to the police. And my man Hendrick Filander says it was all because of his white wife that he got into trouble, and I told Filander I would expect him to do the same for me. Ag, Baas Paul, we all loved Kobie so! Every month he came to Fleur. He never forgot us. He always brought sweets for all the children, and some nights when he played his mouth organ in my father's house we all sang . . . When I married Hendrick Filander, Kobie drove us to the church in his big motor car; and then, as if that was not enough, he brought us this lovely stove all the way from Cape Town in a big lorry and put it into this house. It is just like the stove in the big house at Fleur, Baas Paul."

She opened the oven proudly. "I bake my own bread, and in the winter our house is the warmest in the valley . . . And, Baas Paul, always when Kobie came to Fleur he would talk to Oubaas Gert for hours in the kelder. The Oubaas was lonely, you know. Once when they were walking through the vineyard, Katrina Bruintjies said they looked almost like father and son, and my father gave Katrina a clout. How dare she speak like that about Oubaas Gert? She always had a tongue like a lizard, that one."

It was at that moment that a dam burst inside me. A lifetime of carefully suppressed emotion burst its bonds. I began to shake — a quivering in my belly spreading upward through my chest and down my limbs. My knees and hands shook uncontrollably and my teeth chattered. I felt the icy sweat of shock suffuse my skin.

Sarie's eyes flared wide with alarm. She hesitated only a moment, then folded me in her arms, holding my gibbering face to her warm breast. "Come, Baas Paul, come now."

She supported me as I lurched across the room. I heard the scrape of curtain rings and saw the expanse of the patchwork quilt on the wide bed. There was a squeak of springs as I flopped down. Sarie was kneeling, easing off my shoes. Convulsive tremors tore through my body. I heard Sarie's voice as she crooned over and over, "Ag Baas Paul . . . there Baas Paul . . . never mind, Baas Paul." She was lying next to me, pressing my head to her breast, her thighs stilling my quivering legs.

Hours later, I woke with the toddler plucking at the bedclothes. Beyond the curtain, Sarie was moving about the room. I put out a hand to the child. He flopped to the floor and crawled under the curtain in playful alarm.

I lay there savoring blessed relief. Dr. Paul Pendrake was dead. He had died this morning in the sand at the edge of the airport . . . and I was glad.

Did men, I thought, really wish to be deluded? Paul Pendrake had been slave to a cult of hopeless compromise which not only accepted human baseness, but called that acceptance wisdom; a cult so despairing that it found comfort only in the exploitation of human fear. At what point did the virtue of tolerance merge into the degradation of connivance? What comfort was there in the thought that he was not alone in his delusion? Here in his own country, Paul Pendrake had knowingly tolerated a cult so precarious in its bigotry that the martyrdom of a man like Kobie September was vital to its survival.

Paul Pendrake was better dead. There can be no life without death. Kobie knew, Stompie knew, and George Paku knew. Each had atoned.

But I am alive. I am a man, I am free, and I have a purpose. The Afrikaner Broederbond must be brought to account. That is the least I owe you, Mr. September.

The sunset on the eastern peaks was deepening to mauve as Sarie stood at her cottage door with her child and waved. "Goodbye, Baas Paul! Remember me to Miss Bella, Baas Paul."

I was thoughtful and renewed as I drove up the road. The air was heavy with the breath of ripening vineyards. How I loved the spirit of this valley! For three hundred years my people had lived here in peace and dignity, true to their

191

faith and to the values they brought with them from Europe. What a remarkable place, South Africa!

I swung through the gates of Fleur. There they were on the stoep — the three who had nurtured me and surrounded me with love — Uncle Gert Cilliers leaning heavily on his walking-stick, my mother now white-haired and frail, and Grietjie, shrunken in her wheelchair.

"Paul!" My mother clung to me. "Paul, we have been so anxious. We expected you at noon."

"You expected me?"

"Yes," Uncle Gert said. "Colonel Lategan has been very kind. He has kept us informed."

A ray of the setting sun pierced a cleft in the western peaks. The house glowed golden among her darkening vineyards.

"Look, my Kleinbaas," Grietjie's thin voice piped. "Look, God is saying goodnight to the house."

Author's Note

The term "Baas" is not analogous with the English word "boss." It is used voluntarily and without compulsion as a term of respect and deference. It usually precedes the Christian name and is comparable to the Victorian "master." Kleinbaas: Young Master; Oubaas: Old Master.